"You look right with a baby in your arms,"

Jack said.

Rozlyn felt an ache of emotion fill her throat as she looked down at her friend's child. It would have felt right to have had your baby, Jack, she thought.

"I often thought about you and I having a child," he went on. "But I guess you didn't know that."

His words were a complete surprise. Rozlyn stared at him. "No, I didn't."

Jack's mouth twisted. "I know I didn't have much fathering, and I don't know much of what a father's supposed to be, but I would have loved our child, Roz."

His admission pierced Rozlyn's heart. "I didn't think you wanted to be a father," she murmured.

The tears in her eyes tore at Jack. "You didn't think I wanted to be a husband, either. But I did."

MARRY ME, Cowboy

RODEO RIDER

Stella Bagwell

REUNION WESTERN-STYLE

Silhouette Books

Published by Silhouette Books

America's Publisher of Contemporary Romance

SILHOUETTE BOOKS

ISBN: 0-373-65316-6

RODEO RIDER

Copyright © 1992 by Stella Bagwell

First Silhouette Books printing July 1992

Visit Silhouette Books at www.eHarlequin.com

Printed in U.S.A.

STELLA BAGWELL

sold her first book to Silhouette in November 1985. More than forty novels later, she still loves her job and says she isn't completely content unless she's writing. Recently, she and her husband of thirty years moved from the hills of Oklahoma to Seadrift, Texas, a sleepy little fishing town located on the coastal bend. Stella says the water, the tropical climate and the seabirds make it a lovely place to let her imagination soar and to put the stories in her head down on paper.

She and her husband have one son, Jason, who lives and teaches high school math in nearby Port Lavaca.

To the cowboy,
a true romantic character of the American West.

Chapter One

Jack Barnett reached up with his right hand and gave the brim of his black Stetson hat one hard tug, pulling it tight against his forehead. He flexed the fingers of his left hand between the braided grass rope and the hairy hide of the black Brangus bull that stood motionless beneath him, pinioned by the chute. Adrenaline poured through Jack's veins, heightening his senses. He was acutely aware of the anxious crowd behind him, the smell of the dirt on the arena floor and the power of the animal beneath him.

Time seemed to stop as Jack breathed deeply, filling his lungs, then letting the air out slowly, purging his mind of everything but the eight-second ride before him.

When he was ready, he gave a single nod to the man on the gate. The chute popped open and the Brangus bull exploded out like a wad of dynamite. Jack felt as if his left arm were being wrenched from its socket as the bull's hindquarters reached an incredible height, then slammed back to earth.

Colors and images danced before his vision as he fought to stay aboard the animal. Time stood still. Eight seconds was a long time when you were fighting to stay astride two thousand pounds of angry bull. But at last the buzzer sounded, and Jack knew that once again he'd made it. With a hard yank, he pulled his hand free of the rope and vaulted from the back of the bull. His shoulder hit the soft dirt with a thud before he rolled to his feet.

"Throw some water on the man, boys, 'cause Jack Barnett is hot tonight!" the announcer's voice boomed over the loudspeaker. "And it's gonna show when the judges finish tallying their scorecards!"

Pausing to catch his breath, Jack glanced up at the scoreboard. When the numbers flashed across it, he crammed the black, dusty hat back onto his head and tossed one final look over his shoulder to make sure the pick-up boys had the bull safely away from him.

"Ooo-eee. Eighty-nine points! With a performance like that it's no wonder this man is currently our World Champion Bull Rider," the announcer continued. "And I'd say Jack Barnett is a happy man right about now. I know he's made the fans here in San Antonio tonight appreciate what great athletes we have here at the rodeo."

The coliseum roared with thunderous applause as

Jack exited the arena. Behind the bucking chutes, cowboys thronged around him, eager to slap his back and praise his ride. He acknowledged each one before heading down an earthen-packed alleyway that would take him outside the building.

Jack Barnett is a happy man. The announcer's words echoed once again in Jack's mind and put a wry twist to the corners of his mouth. Maybe riding a notoriously famous bull and winning several thousand dollars for his effort should make him happy. But did it? He'd won more money than any other bull rider in the Professional Rodeo Cowboys Association, giving him the prized position of world champion. Yet now that he'd reached the top, was he really happy?

The question was still lingering in Jack's mind as he stepped from the building and out into the night air. San Antonio was unusually cool this January night, and he hunched his shoulders against the sharp wind as he made his way through the parked vehicles at the back of the coliseum. The cowbell on the bull rigging he'd thrown over his shoulder clanked with the slow rhythm of his walk. It was a lonesome sound to Jack. One that he never heard until the roar of the crowd died away, his ride was over, and he was alone again in some dark parking lot such as this one.

"Jack, is that you?"

He turned abruptly at the sound of his name and squinted at the shadows made by the endless lines of cattle trucks and horse trailers. The voice was familiar, but he couldn't quite pinpoint the identity of its owner.

During his travels on the rodeo circuit, he'd met many people. Too many for Jack to keep straight in his memory.

A figure stepped forward out of the shadows, and Jack stared in stunned surprise at the face. "Michael! What are you doing here?"

The young man dressed in Western clothes and tan felt hat grinned and shrugged his shoulders as though he'd been caught dunking his finger in the sugar bowl. "I'm riding horses, Jack. Gonna ride tomorrow in the slack."

Jack stared in total disbelief at the young man. "The hell you say," he finally managed to get out.

Michael's grin was both broad and sheepish. "Yeah, I'm in the bareback. And you know what, Jack? There's only been a seventy-nine scored so far."

Excitement laced his words, but Jack hardly noticed the kid's enthusiasm. His mind was whirling at the implication of Michael's news.

"I don't suppose Rozlyn is here with you?"

It was a crazy thing to ask, Jack thought. Rozlyn hated rodeoing. But if there was the slightest chance that his estranged wife was here with her brother, he wanted to know.

"Heck, no!" Michael answered with a great deal of fervor. "She was spitting fire the last time I saw her. You know Rozlyn, Jack. She don't want me doing anything like this. She wants me there on the ranch. The Broken Spur is all she cares about—"

Jack's mind continued to race a mile a minute. Michael had left the Broken Spur to rodeo? God, he could just imagine what Rozlyn's reaction had been. Spitting fire was probably an understatement. What was she doing for help back on the ranch? he wondered. Trying to do it all herself? Or did she have another man in her life now? But that wasn't likely, he thought. Otherwise she would have contacted him about getting a divorce.

"So you've left the ranch," Jack said as he struggled to control his churning thoughts. "Who's on the ranch with Rozlyn now?"

The younger man tugged at the brim of his hat. Clearly Jack's question made him uncomfortable. "Well, just Grandpa Axton. But Roz is all right, Jack. Heck, she's a lot better at taking care of horses and cows than I am."

Jack looked blankly out over the parking lot. In his wildest dreams he'd never expected to see his young brother-in-law again, or at least not here at the San Antonio rodeo. Michael was a piece of the past Jack had struggled to forget. But now the past was rising up, sending his emotions spinning in a vicious whirlwind.

"Jack? Are you listening, buddy?"

Michael's voice penetrated his abstraction and he looked back at the younger man. "Yeah. I'm listening."

"I asked if you wanta go get a drink?"

Feeling as if he could hardly refuse, Jack nodded. "My truck is right over here. We'll take it."

As the two men worked their way through the parked vehicles, Jack could feel Michael on his heels. He had all sorts of questions, but he pushed them aside until they were seated in his pickup. Even then he turned his attention to starting the engine and switching on the heater.

On the other end of the wide seat, Michael blew on his hands and shuffled his feet. Jack knew the young man was just twenty-one. He'd only been seventeen when Jack and Rozlyn had married, and barely nineteen when they'd parted. But during that time the two of them had grown close. Without conceit, Jack knew Michael idolized him. The boy had never kept it a secret that he wanted to be a rodeo performer. It looked as though Michael was finally out trying to realize his dream.

"It sure is cold down here," Michael remarked as Jack headed the truck out onto the street. "You still living in Houston?"

"Yes."

"You—have another woman now?"

"No."

A few moments of awkward silence passed and Jack wondered what the young man was thinking. Was he speculating if Jack had left his sister in order to have a free rein with other women?

"Roz doesn't have a man either. Hell, she won't even look at other men."

Jack wasn't sure how he felt about this news. He had to admit a small part of him was relieved, but things might be better if Rozlyn had found another man.

Michael continued in spite of Jack's lack of response. "I asked her if it was because she still loves you, but Roz says it's because you ruined her as far as men are concerned."

Jack supposed he had. Still, Rozlyn had managed to ruin just about every dream, every hope he'd ever had. But Jack didn't want to think of that. He'd just won one of the biggest rodeos of the year. He was going to be happy even if it killed him.

"How's Axton?" Jack asked, deliberately changing the subject.

"He's pretty feeble," Michael answered. "He has to use a cane now—because of his arthritis. But his mind is as sharp as ever."

Since Michael and Rozlyn's grandfather was in his eighties, Jack figured a sharp mind was plenty to be thankful for. "That's good to hear."

After that both men remained quiet until Jack pulled into a fast-food restaurant. Michael looked around in bewilderment.

"I thought we were going to get a drink?"

"We are," Jack answered. "I want a cup of coffee."

Michael's expression changed to a comical mixture of disgust and disbelief. "Coffee? I thought rodeo cowboys liked Jack Daniel's. Or something a damn smart stouter than coffee!"

Jack grimaced at the stereotype Michael was referring to. He knew many people thought of rodeo riders as hard drinkers. Men who were reckless in both their work and play. But more often than not that description was far from the truth. "Not if the cowboy is serious about being an athlete."

"Hell, Jack, I am serious! But you're forgetting I'm a grown man. I'd like to drink a few beers and do a little dancing if you don't mind."

Jack was torn between laughing and scolding the boy. "I do mind. And I don't want to hear another curse word out of you. Roz hates it when you curse."

"How do you know? You haven't lived with us for two years or better."

"That doesn't mean I've lost my memory."

Jack pushed through the double glass doors and found an empty booth at the back. Michael took a seat opposite him, then grimaced as Jack ordered two coffees from the hovering waitress.

"It sure is good running into you like this," Michael said when the waitress left to get the coffee. "I left Llano about three weeks ago and have been looking for you ever since. But I figured you'd have to be here in San Antonio. Guess I figured right, didn't I?"

A wry smile curved the corners of Jack's mouth. It was good to see Roz's brother again, but the whole idea of Michael leaving Rozlyn and the Broken Spur was unsettling Jack pretty thoroughly. He knew how much Rozlyn loved and depended on her brother. Now she was all alone. Maybe that shouldn't matter to him. But try as he might, Jack couldn't remain totally callous toward Rozlyn.

"Yeah. You figured right about that," Jack told him. "But when did you get the idea of leaving home? My Lord, boy, Roz needs you."

Michael shook his head determinedly. "No, she needed you, Jack. And you walked out on her."

Jack's stoic expression didn't change as he pulled off his hat and placed it on the vinyl seat beside him. "Your sister didn't leave me much choice, Michael."

The young man's handsome face was set with a bit of defiance as he looked across the table at Jack. "Roz said you left because you didn't want the responsibility of marriage or children. She said you were just like your dad was."

Jack winced inwardly at the mention of his father. Tom Barnett had walked away from his problems and responsibilities when Jack had only been thirteen years old. He'd never seen his father since. To have Rozlyn compare him to the man was bitter as hell.

"And what do you think, Michael? You agree with her?"

Michael's face was touched with sadness as he shook his head. "Aw, Jack, I don't blame you for staying away. I know how Roz is. She—well, she means well, and I love her. But she's just so damn stubborn."

Jack knew all too well just how stubborn Rozlyn could be. After all, he'd spent more than two years trying to get her to see things from his perspective. He'd never succeeded.

"So you've been riding broncs," Jack said, carefully steering the conversation away from Rozlyn. "Have you been winning?"

Michael's eyes remained on the tabletop. "A little. I won a fifth at South Dakota."

"And that gave you enough money to buy your gas and entry fees down here," Jack said with pointed resignation.

Michael looked up, his expression suddenly defensive. "Well, I haven't expected to win every rodeo I entered. Even you didn't do that, Jack. I remember you telling me it took you at least a year to start making money."

Jack leaned back in the seat, cradling his coffee cup in one hand. "I'm not trying to put you down, Michael. Frankly, what's got me wondering is your sister. How is she managing things without your help?"

Michael ducked his head. "Roz doesn't need me," he mumbled. "Besides, she can't understand that I want to rodeo. She thinks I should be like her, and want to hole myself up on that damn ranch. You know her, Jack. The Broken Spur is all she thinks about."

Jack did know. The tradition of family and the legacy of land meant everything to Rozlyn. Jack himself didn't have much faith in either. His parents had lost their ranch when he'd been just a boy, and the troubles that followed had eventually led to their divorce.

"Has she hired anyone to help her?" Jack persisted.

Michael shrugged. "Not that I know of. Every time I call her, she starts lecturing, so I haven't called in several days."

Jack shook his head. "She needs you, Michael."

Michael shook his head back at Jack. "No, it's *you* she needs, Jack. She has ever since you left."

Jack gazed out the plate-glass window as Michael's words dredged up bittersweet memories of his marriage with Rozlyn. Mostly he didn't believe Rozlyn had ever needed or wanted him. He couldn't imagine her needing him now. But Michael's words bothered him just the same.

"You always were a dreamer, Michael. Sounds like you haven't changed."

The younger man set his coffee cup down with a hard thud. "I'll tell you one thing, Jack. I'm determined not to waste my life the way Roz is wasting hers."

"You call helping your sister a waste?" Jack was riled even though he had no right to be. Michael was a grown man now. It wasn't written anywhere that he had to live his life on the Broken Spur.

"Hell, yes, it's a waste. Roz is working herself to death just because the Broken Spur was handed down through the family to us. If you ask me, there's more to life than family tradition."

Jack's edgy temper was suddenly replaced by an unbearable sadness. "You think so, huh?"

Michael nodded vigorously. "I sure do. That's why I want to be just like you, Jack."

* * *

That's why I want to be just like you, Jack.

As Jack drove through the Texas hill country, Michael's words continued to play over in his mind. Since their conversation last night, Jack had tried to put his young brother-in-law out of his thoughts. But in spite of all his trying, it had been impossible to dismiss what the boy had said to him, or the guilt that Jack had felt upon hearing it.

It was the guilt, he told himself, that had made him toss his things into his truck and head north to Llano and to Rozlyn. Even though he wasn't directly responsible for Michael's decision to leave the Broken Spur, he knew he was a major reason for it. Michael had always considered Jack his hero. But Jack wasn't a hero. Neither was he a role model. Yet Michael was following in his footsteps, right down to walking out on Rozlyn.

The hills Jack was traveling through began to flatten somewhat. Wind-whipped mesquite trees took the place of cedar, giving the land a faded, desolate look. The area was familiar to him even though he'd only called this area home for two years. But Jack Barnett had forgotten nothing about the place, or the woman he was going to see. He'd pushed it to the back of his mind, but he'd never forgotten. Now memories rushed at him like an oncoming freight train, some pleasant, some painful, pushing his mind one way and then the other.

When he entered the outskirts of Llano, he slowed the truck while his sharp gray eyes took a quick survey of the shops and stores and the handful of people going to and from. He'd left many friends and a piece of his life behind in this small Texas town. He hadn't thought he'd missed it. Until now.

Glancing down at the gas gauge, Jack noted the marker was showing nearly empty, so he geared down the pickup and pulled over at a familiar gas station.

A brown leather jacket was lying on the seat beside him. He slipped it on and was stepping down from the truck just as a tall, lanky man came from the building.

"What can I do for you, sir?"

"Fill it up, Jim Bob."

At the sound of his name, the station attendant took another glance at the man in the black Stetson and expensive jacket. "Jack Barnett? Is that you?"

The comical look of surprise on Jim Bob's face had Jack laughing as he extended a hand to the man. "Sure is. How are you, buddy?"

"Well, gosh dog!" Jim Bob exclaimed, giving Jack's hand a hearty pump. "If this ain't something, seein' you back here in Llano! You drivin' through?"

The station attendant reached for the nozzle on the pump. Once he had the gas pumping into the truck, his round eyes kept darting from the clicking numbers to Jack.

"No. I'm here to see Rozlyn," Jack answered, then thought how insane that sounded. From the look of surprise on Jim Bob's face, the station attendant thought so, too.

The man's reaction made Jack realize that people

around here might view him as a bastard who'd run out on his wife. But it hadn't been that way. At least not in Jack's mind. Or his heart.

"I heard Michael's taken up riding broncs," Jim Bob spoke up. "Guess he thinks he can make some of that easy money."

Jack smiled faintly as he shook his head. "It's not that easy, Jim Bob. I can testify to that."

"Bet you can at that," Jim Bob agreed. "And young Michael needs to understand that money isn't everything."

Jack reached for his wallet and pulled out two bills. Jim Bob took them and started toward the building. Jack followed to get the change.

"You're right, Jim Bob. Money isn't everything," Jack told him as the two men entered the warmth of the building.

Behind a small, dusty counter, Jim Bob punched open an old cash register and pulled out several bills. "Well, I guess you've made your share of money riding those rodeo bulls."

"I guess I have," Jack replied as Jim Bob handed him the change. But what had money done for him? he wondered a bit ruefully. He hadn't made many changes in his life since it started pouring in. And the money certainly hadn't made Rozlyn come running back to him. Money wasn't something that counted for much with her.

Obviously impressed, Jim Bob shook his head.

"You must be pretty brave or pretty crazy to get on those things."

Jack chuckled. "A little of the first and a whole lot of the last." He put the bills away and jammed the wallet back into his jeans. "I'd better get on out to the ranch. See y'all round, Jim Bob."

"Thanks, Jack. And you tell Rozlyn hi for me now."

"I'll do that," Jack said, climbing into the truck. He hoped she'd give him a chance to talk at all. He had a lot he wanted to say. Mainly, why he'd come back to the ranch, although he doubted she would understand his explanation. She hadn't understood why he had left two years before, and he didn't think she'd understand his need to make sure she was all right now that Michael was gone. He wasn't sure he understood it himself.

"Darn it, Blue Jeans! I said hold still!"

Rozlyn grabbed the dangling lead rope attached to the gray horse's halter and pulled the animal forward. The horse snorted and danced sideways in the small stall, but Rozlyn somehow managed to steady him.

"I know the medicine burns," she told the horse as she looped the lead rope around a board on the stall. Once it was secure, she stroked the animal's neck, then crooned to him softly, "Here boy, I know it hurts, darlin'. But you have to have medicine on it, or it will eventually hurt even more."

Jack watched her from the shadows just inside the

door of the barn. It was a bittersweet feeling for him to see Rozlyn at work. She'd always been passionate about the ranch and the animals on it. It showed now in her caring movements, the concentration on her face, and her patience when the animal tried to jerk his foot away.

Eventually Rozlyn managed to swab the deep cuts around the hairline at the hoof with a brown liquid that filled the barn with the pungent smell of turpentine. After she'd pushed the dabber back into the medicine bottle and removed the halter from the horse, Jack decided it was time to make his presence known.

Pushing away from the door, he moved slowly forward, his lithe steps silent on the sawdust beneath his boots.

"Hello, Roz."

Startled by the sound of his voice, Rozlyn spun around to see him standing in the alleyway of the barn. The dim glow of a bare light bulb hanging from the rafters illuminated him with a pale yellow halo. Her mouth fell open, then just as quickly snapped shut.

"Damn it, Jack!"

His lips twitched as his eyes drank in the sight of her. She was dressed in old jeans and boots with a red plaid shirt buttoned over thermal underwear. Her long, naturally curly hair had been pulled into a single braid, but the biggest part of it had worked loose and was now falling about her face in a cascade of chestnut curls. Her wide-set eyes, which were a mixture of blue and green, had taken on a hardness that bored right through him.

One corner of his mouth curved in a wry smile. "Damn it because I scared you, or damn it because I'm here?"

"Both," she said, tight-lipped.

Behind her, the big gray horse moved restlessly around the stall. It would have been easy for Jack to go soothe the animal. He knew the right thing to do for a horse. Yet he'd always been at a loss as to how to deal with Rozlyn, how to soothe her temper, her doubts and fears.

He took a step toward her. "Sorry on both counts," he said, not really sounding sorry at all.

Rozlyn didn't move. She couldn't. She felt as if her knees were on the verge of buckling. She'd never expected to see her husband again. At least not here on the Broken Spur. "What are you doing here?" she asked.

Jack's eyes remained fastened on her face. It seemed like ages since he'd seen her delicate features, since he'd touched them with his fingers and his lips. But then it *had* been ages.

"I ran into Michael last night," he said.

"Is he in trouble?" Rozlyn asked quickly, fear for her brother's safety overriding the initial shock of seeing her husband again.

Jack shook his head. "Not any that I'm aware of."

She sighed with obvious relief, then lifted her hands to push impatiently at the unruly curls in her eyes.

"Thank God for that. What does he want? Did he send you to get more money out of me?"

Jack's brows lifted with surprise. "Money?" he repeated blankly. "I'm not here on Michael's behalf."

Rozlyn's expression was instantly wary. "Then exactly what are you doing here?"

"We *are* still married, Rozlyn."

The faint arrogance in his voice caused Rozlyn's eyes to widen, her chin to lift. Did he actually think she needed reminding? Being married to Jack Barnett was something she never forgot.

"That doesn't answer my question," she said.

Jack shrugged with a casualness that irked Rozlyn. "Let's just say I thought it was time I came back," he said evasively.

And what was that supposed to mean? she wondered. That he'd simply decided he wanted to be her husband again? Or had he come back to ask her for a divorce?

Rozlyn's eyes narrowed skeptically as they glided over him. At thirty-one, Jack Barnett was a perfect specimen of prime male. His leather jacket covered a set of thick, broad shoulders that tapered down to a trim waist. His thighs were long and sinewy, as were his arms. Straining against the force of a two-thousand-pound bull had honed them to rock hardness and incredible strength. She didn't have to take off his hat to know she'd find a thick head of dark blond hair, some of it streaked lighter by the sun. And she wouldn't have to step closer to see the hard lines and angles of his face, the sensuous lips, the gray eyes with their thick brown lashes. His features had been permanently etched into her memory, a memory that she sometimes wished she could pour from her mind like a pitcher of water.

Jack could feel Rozlyn's resentful gaze traveling over him. In turn he examined her. He had no idea what his wife was seeing in him, but Jack was seeing a tall, slender woman with high rounded breasts, a tiny waist, full hips and long, strong legs. Beneath the work clothes, her skin would be ivory white, soft and smooth with a sprinkling of freckles across her shoulders and arms.

He'd always thought Rozlyn beautiful. Now he was seeing for himself that her beauty had not faded or changed from the image he'd carried in his mind.

"*You* thought it was about time to come back," she said mockingly. "That's something, Jack. It really is."

Her sarcasm had him grinding his teeth. "I know you never considered this ranch my home, too. But from what Michael told me—"

"Michael's chosen his own way. If he's afraid I'm going to hound him about it anymore, he doesn't have to worry. I've accepted the fact that I can't change him. No more than I could ever change you." Deciding she'd said all she wanted to say, she stepped past him toward the open barn door. "And now I have work to do," she tossed coolly over her shoulder.

Jack balled his hands into tight fists inside his jacket. Drawing in a deep breath, he forced himself to relax. He'd sworn he wasn't going to let Rozlyn get to him.

With long, purposeful strides, he followed her out of the barn. He found her at the west end of the old building, loading a pickup with bales of alfalfa hay.

Before Rozlyn realized he was anywhere near, Jack walked up behind her and plucked the iron hay hook from her hand. "If you think you can dismiss me, then act as though I'm no longer here, you're greatly mistaken."

The cool assurance of his words made Rozlyn whirl around and pierce him with a glare. "Look, Jack, maybe you should just tell me what you're doing here."

His jaw clenched at her abruptness. "I'm here because I know that Michael has left the ranch. That he's no longer here to help you."

For a second Jack thought he saw a shadow of pain flicker across her face. But maybe he had only imagined it because he wanted to believe there was still a vulnerable spot in her.

"Of course he's not here to help me! He believes he can become a famous bronc rider. So he's out chasing that elusive dream. Just like you, Jack."

Jack's expression was mocking as he turned and stabbed the iron hook into a bale of green alfalfa. "I wouldn't call it elusive, Rozlyn. I've managed to make a decent living at it. Some people even call me a success."

He flipped the hay bale onto the pickup bed, then

glanced back at Rozlyn. She looked bitter. But that didn't surprise him. His chosen profession had come between them almost from the beginning of their marriage.

"That doesn't mean Michael can be what you are. He doesn't have your skill, Jack. I don't think he ever will."

Jack was surprised at her words, even though she hadn't necessarily meant them as a compliment. Rozlyn had rarely acknowledged his ability as a bull rider. He found it ironic that she was doing so now.

"He'll have to discover that for himself, Roz. It's a part of finding himself as a man."

Not waiting for her to make a reply, Jack reached for another bale of hay. Rozlyn found herself watching his strong, graceful movements as he shoved the bale onto the pickup bed. No man had ever stirred her as Jack had. Even the bitterness in her heart could not erase the erotic images his lovemaking had left behind. Jack had been a wonderful lover. Whenever he'd been home, her angry thoughts tacked on.

"You should feel good, Jack," she felt compelled to say. "While we were married you made a deep impression on Michael. He scoffs at family values and views the open road as an invitation to paradise."

Anger at her unfairness knifed through Jack. He'd never scoffed at family values. It was more that he didn't know anything about them. His parents had divorced when he was thirteen. When his mother remarried, she'd left Jack with his dad. But Tom Barnett had been a broken, disillusioned man, and one day he'd simply walked off and never come back.

Jack had eventually been taken in by an aunt and uncle, but he'd never fully gotten over the abandonment of his parents, or the feeling of being unloved and unwanted.

"Look, Roz," he said, forcing his thoughts back to the present. "I didn't come here to talk about Michael's future. I came here to work—to help you."

Rozlyn was stunned and it showed all over her face. "Work?" she repeated, then laughed as though she found that idea hilarious. "I can't really see you missing even one rodeo. Besides, I don't have the extra income to hire help."

Jack went rigid with anger. "Don't insult me with the mention of money! I'm your husband."

Rozlyn's laugh was short and caustic. "Oh, yeah? Since when?"

Too angry to care if he answered or not, Rozlyn turned to climb into the cab of the truck. As she was about to slam the door behind her, Jack's fingers clamped down on her upper arm.

"Since now!" he bit out. "And I'm telling you, Rozlyn, you are going to accept my help, whether you like it or not."

She twisted around, defiant words on her tongue. Yet they quickly dissolved as she looked into his angry gray eyes. Her heart began to race in erratic little lurches. The feel of Jack's hand on her arm was the last thing she should be thinking about. And yet, in truth, it was the only thing she *could* think about.

Taking a bracing breath, she tried her best to ignore his nearness. "I'm not a charity case, Jack. I don't know what Michael's been spouting off to you, but this ranch is doing fine. I'm doing fine. There's no need for this grand gesture of yours." Rozlyn knew the last thing he could possibly really want to do was stay here on the ranch and help her. Jack was a cowboy. If he wasn't on the road to the next rodeo he was miserable. It was the very thing that had driven them apart.

Jack loosened his grip on her arm, but he couldn't quite make himself remove his hand completely. "I'm not trying to be your knight in white armor, Roz. God knows that I couldn't be that anyway."

Roz wondered what he meant by that, but she wasn't about to ask. Right now she had to get away from him before she shattered into a million pieces.

"Look, Jack, I have feeding to do, and Axton will be hungry for supper." Hearing her voice start to quaver, she quickly looked away from him. "If you want a thank-you for your offer, then thank you. But I'm doing all right by myself."

As soon as she spoke the last word, Rozlyn slammed the door of the cab. She stepped down on the gas pedal and the truck shot away from him. Driving away might be the coward's way out, but Rozlyn didn't want Jack to see what his showing up here again was doing to her. She was shaking all over and acrid tears stung her throat and eyes.

How dared he come back? After all this time he should know she didn't want or need him anymore!

The old pickup rattled and shook as Rozlyn continued to jostle over the rough pasture. Ahead of her was a dry arroyo. What little bit of ruts she'd been following had been washed away by a recent gully washer. She pushed in the clutch and the gears ground together as she shoved the floor shift down so that the pickup could climb to higher, flatter ground.

Rozlyn's movements were automatic, done without conscious thought. Her mind was consumed with Jack. She didn't believe he'd come back to the Broken Spur just to help her out now that Michael was gone. Maybe he *was* back to ask her for a divorce. Maybe he thought he could soften her up with his offer of help so she wouldn't feel inclined to ask for alimony. Especially now that he'd gotten into big-time money, she thought sourly. Whatever the reason, she knew for certain she wasn't ready to deal with Jack Barnett again.

A sharp, biting wind stung Jack's face as he watched Rozlyn and the old green truck move along a narrow track leading into a stand of mesquite trees. It wasn't until it disappeared from sight that he turned and headed to the old stuccoed ranch house.

When Jack entered the back door he was immediately assaulted with memories. He saw Rozlyn everywhere he looked. In the same tartan plaid furniture, the waxed hardwood floors, the African violets blooming at the windowsill.

The kitchen was a mess, which was typical of Rozlyn. She had always hated cooking and the cleaning up that followed. But in all fairness he knew that Rozlyn probably didn't have much time to spend in the kitchen—or any part of the house, for that matter. Especially now that winter was in full swing and everything with four legs and a mouth required feeding. With Michael gone, her work load must be doubled. It was a burden Jack didn't want on Rozlyn's shoulders. But then, he'd never wanted the burden of this ranch on her shoulders at all.

The faint sound of a television could be heard at the back of the house, where a den had been built several years ago. Jack found Rozlyn's grandfather there, sitting in a wooden rocker by the fireplace. An open Bible was in his lap, while on the television screen, a talk-show host was discussing promiscuous sex with a guest panel.

Smiling to himself, Jack entered the room. "Hello, Axton."

The old man didn't appear to be startled by the unexpected sound of Jack's voice. Jack figured that by the time a person reached the age of eighty-five, there wasn't much scare left in them.

Axton eyed Jack over long and hard before he finally spoke. "Well, son, you've finally come back."

Axton had always called Jack *son*. He couldn't remember once during the time he'd lived with this family that the old man had called him Jack. A wry smile twisted his lips at the thought. At least Axton wasn't calling him a worthless bastard.

He went over and shook Axton's gnarled hand, then pulled up a matching rocker. "How have you been, Axton? It's been a long time," he said, noting the deep lines and sallow skin on the man's face.

Axton nodded. "I'm tolerable. It's Rozlyn that worries me."

Rozlyn's grandfather had never been one to tiptoe around whatever was on his mind. Obviously he hadn't changed since Jack had been away. "And why is that?" Jack prompted.

Pondering the question, Axton reached up and rubbed his bushy eyebrows. "She's been right torn up over Michael's leaving. I've told her not to worry about the boy. He has to spread his wings sometimes."

Jack nodded his agreement. In spite of the tough, indifferent act Rozlyn had given him earlier at the barn, Jack knew how close she had always been to her younger brother. And he knew what Michael's leaving must have cost her. "And what does Rozlyn say to that?" Jack asked him.

Axton's eyes settled back on the Bible in his lap. "She doesn't see it that way. She thinks he could have spread his wings right here in Llano."

Jack had gotten that same impression from the few words Rozlyn had tossed at him. "I take it she thinks Michael is wasting his life trying to make it on the rodeo circuit."

Axton lifted his gaze back up to Jack. "Why son,

you should have known she would. She wanted him to be interested in the Broken Spur and to help her build it up again to what it was back in the fifties, when me and Rosa were going strong. Michael thinks she's dreaming and Rozlyn thinks her brother is foolin' himself. And crazy or not, she thinks because you've done so well for yourself riding those bulls that you encouraged Michael even more.''

Jack shook his head. ''Last night in San Antonio was the first time I'd seen Michael since I left this ranch two years ago. I had no idea what he was up to. And I sure wasn't trying to lure him away from here, if that's what she thinks.''

Axton let out a heavy sigh. ''No, I don't expect you did try that. But you see—Roz is—well, she's bitter. She feels pretty deserted now. First by you, and now by Michael.''

Jack had never felt as if he'd deserted Rozlyn. It was more like she'd pushed him out of her life. But there was no use hashing over the issue with Axton. The old man had always been fair with him. Jack couldn't ask for more than that.

''I want to help Rozlyn. This ranch is too much for her to take care of now that Michael is gone.''

''That's true. 'Twas while Michael was still here.'' After carefully marking his place in the Bible with a red ribbon, Axton closed the worn book. ''Did you see her, tell her you want to help?''

Grimacing at the memory of their encounter, Jack nodded. ''She wasn't too pleased about the offer. But

I didn't expect her to be happy to see me. So it wasn't a surprise.''

A frown wrinkled Axton's face even more. "Oh, hell, son, I'll never believe that you or Rozlyn really wanted to live apart. You were both just too blind and stubborn to bend.''

With a tired sigh, Jack leaned back in the rocker and closed his eyes. Instantly he was reliving the last horrendous fight that had led up to his leaving. Rozlyn had given him the ultimatum of quitting rodeo or quitting their marriage.

Jack had been so hurt and angry he'd lashed back at her, accusing her of caring only for herself and her own needs, not his. He'd never been able to make her understand why he needed to travel around the country riding dangerous bulls. She could never see that it was the one thing in his life he felt confident about and that he could excel at. He'd wanted so badly for her to share his accomplishment in the sport, to be proud of him. But instead of encouraging him to use his talents, she'd accused him of wanting to be a drifter instead of a family man.

In the end it was a fight that had taken them both too far for either one to back down. Rather than face a divorce, Jack had simply walked out. He'd hit the rodeo circuit with a vengeance and refused to let Rozlyn weigh on his heart. She'd made her choice. She wanted the Broken Spur more than she'd ever wanted him. That much had been obvious to Jack when time passed and she'd never showed up or tried to contact him.

Chapter Two

It was after dark when Rozlyn returned to the ranch house. By then a slow drizzle had begun to fall. She ran through the rain to the back porch and quickly entered the warmth of the kitchen.

As soon as she stepped inside the room, the smell of cooking food hit her. She stared disbelievingly over at the gas range, where Jack was forking pieces of fried chicken onto a platter.

The sight of him cooking didn't surprise Rozlyn, but she *was* surprised to find he was still on the ranch. Jack Barnett wasn't a stayer. He'd proved that when he'd walked out on their marriage.

"What are you doing here?" she blurted before she realized she'd formed the words.

Jack looked around to see her slipping out of her jacket. She tossed it at a chair, but it missed and slipped to the floor. Instead of going to retrieve it, she stood staring at him, her hands planted on either side of her waist, her expression challenging.

"I'm cooking. What does it look like?" he answered calmly.

"You're supposed to be gone!" Rozlyn countered, his casual attitude fanning the flames of her temper. "I told you—"

"Leave the boy be!"

Both Rozlyn and Jack turned. Axton was thumping into the kitchen with the aid of a walking cane.

Rozlyn groaned aloud at her grandfather's interference. "Pa, you don't understand. I told Jack earlier that—"

Axton glared at his granddaughter as he continued to shuffle into the room. "The man has cooked supper, Sis. I think that gives him a right to eat it, don't you?"

Knowing it would be futile to keep arguing with her grandfather, Rozlyn let out a long breath and left the room. Down the hall in the bathroom, she closed the door and pulled off her shirt. After sluicing her face with warm water, she blotted it dry with a towel, then stared into the medicine-chest mirror.

She saw a pale face, eyes lined with fatigue, and a cheek that had been scratched by chaparral while she'd been hunting for a newborn calf. She didn't care. She just wanted to yell with frustration. This past month had been a bad one. Michael had left for the unknown, the bad weather had taken its toll on her herd, and now Jack was back. It was almost too much for her to bear.

Yet she *would* bear it, she fiercely promised herself as she headed to her bedroom. She wasn't going to dissolve into tears and give Jack the impression she needed him. For the past two years she'd kept this ranch afloat without him. That should tell him how much she needed him!

After changing into clean jeans and a sweater, she went back to the kitchen. Jack and her grandfather were already seated at the table and deep in conversation when she entered the room. Both men went suddenly quiet as they became aware of her presence. Rozlyn could only suppose they'd been discussing her, and she groaned inwardly at the thought of the personal things her grandfather was more than likely telling Jack.

She took her usual seat and tried not to notice that Jack was sitting directly across from her. Axton said a short prayer and began to pass the food around the table.

"I see you haven't forgotten how to cook, son," Axton said.

Jack looked up to see the old man chomp into a drumstick. The sight brought an amused curve to Jack's lips. He'd never known Axton to wear his false teeth unless he made a trip into Llano.

"I'm not so sure about that, Axton," he replied. "It's been a long time since I've had time to eat anything that I couldn't hold in my hand. Much less cook it.''

Axton grunted his disbelief. ''Don't know how you young men live such fast lives. Guess you made it up to the Calgary Stampede this year?''

Jack nodded, then winked at the old man. ''You should let me take you up there sometime, Axton. It's a sight to see.''

Axton chuckled. ''Son, it would be a sight to get me more than ten miles from this ranch, much less a thousand or two.''

Jack laughed along with him. ''Why, a thousand miles is just a little jump, Axton. I've traveled more than a hundred thousand this past year and it hasn't hurt me.''

Rozlyn didn't want to hear about his fast life on the rodeo circuit. That life had torn their marriage apart. ''I found a new calf this evening. A heifer,'' she said in an attempt to change the conversation. ''That's the third one this week.''

Jack glanced her way, his eyes lingering on her soft pink lips. ''The weather is taking a turn for the worse. Did you bring the calf and mother in?''

Rozlyn bristled. How dared he show up here after two years and have the gall to question her about the ranch's welfare! Did he honestly think his opinion mattered to her now, after all this time?

She moistened her lips with her tongue and prayed he'd quit looking at her. ''No, Jack, I didn't.''

''This cold rain will be hard on a newborn,'' he said

easily, giving Rozlyn the impression that her waspish voice hadn't stung him at all.

When she turned a hard look on him, however, he merely lifted his eyebrows in arrogant anticipation.

"How was I supposed to bring her and the baby back here without a trailer?" she asked.

"All you had to do was put the calf in the back of the truck and mama would have followed."

"Sure. And how, pray tell me, was I going to get it to the truck without her trying to run me over?" she asked tersely.

Their eyes clashed and Rozlyn felt heat rush from somewhere deep inside her straight to her face. She wanted to hurt Jack—to humiliate him for all the pain, the loneliness and uncertainty he'd caused in her life. But there was also a crazy, unbidden part of her that wanted to touch him, feel his hard body against hers. The realization shook her, causing her hand to tremble as she reached for her water glass.

"Forget about that little heifer," Axton told his granddaughter, "and hand me the gravy. I had to go all day without a thing to eat."

Rozlyn managed to pull her eyes away from Jack and look down the table at her grandfather. "And why was that, Pa?" she asked, forcing herself to be calm and patient.

Other than Michael, Axton was the only family she had left. Her parents had been killed in a flash flood when she'd been only sixteen. The accident had devastated Rozlyn, and it had forced her to grow up virtually overnight. Sometimes it was difficult for Rozlyn to remember what it was like to have been a child without any worries or responsibilities on her shoulders.

"There wasn't a thing in the kitchen without salt or cholesterol. You know I'm not supposed to have those two things, Rozlyn."

She motioned toward the bowl of gravy. "I suppose you think that has no salt or cholesterol in it?"

Axton ladled the white gravy onto his plate as though a health-conscious diet was the least of his concerns. "The boy was good enough to cook. That makes me good enough to eat."

Rozlyn resisted the urge to roll her eyes heavenward and dipped her fork into the mashed potatoes and gravy on her plate. She had to concede that Jack was a good cook. It was one of the things he'd always done better than her. But then Jack had been good at a lot of things. Except being a responsible husband, she thought.

Desperate to get her mind off Jack, she looked to her grandfather. "If it's not raining, I'd like to move the herd in the west section over to the middle section. They've grazed the pasture they're in completely bare."

Jack studied her covertly from his lowered lashes. Exhaustion shadowed her eyes, and her cheeks were still flushed brightly from being out in the cold wind all day. She was trying to do the work of two men, and he figured it was probably an effort for her just to raise the fork to her mouth.

Rozlyn had hurt him in the past. Yet even so, seeing her like this tore at Jack. He wanted to reach out and touch her face, draw her into his arms and hold her tight. They were dangerous feelings, he knew, but ones that he couldn't seem to push aside.

"I can be ready to ride by daylight," he found himself saying.

Jack's deep voice pulled at Rozlyn's senses, but she refused to let her eyes meet his. "I'm sure there's a rodeo out there you need to be at by tomorrow night," she said dryly.

From the corner of her vision, she could see her grandfather scowling at her. That didn't surprise Rozlyn. He'd always been partial to Jack. Two years ago when Jack had left the ranch for the last time, her grandfather had exploded. He'd accused Rozlyn of misunderstanding Jack, of wanting and expecting too much from him. Rozlyn had wound up feeling deserted by both men. She still felt that way.

"They'll manage to have it without me, Roz," Jack told her.

"You'd have them cattle moved twice as fast with Jack helping you," Axton quickly spoke up.

Rozlyn didn't reply. Instead she focused her attention back on her plate. Actually, she didn't know what to say. It was true she needed help badly, and no one knew that any better than Axton. But didn't her grandfather realize what having Jack around would do to her? After a few days she'd be torn into emotional shreds.

Conversation was sparse and strained during the remainder of the meal. Axton was the first to push his plate away.

"That was good, son. Hadn't had cooking like that in a long time. You never did tell me where you learned how. It sure wasn't from Rozlyn. She hates the kitchen."

Jack's smile was vacant. "I learned a long time ago, Axton, from my aunt. She and Uncle Vernon expected me to earn my keep."

"Guess I'd forgotten about you being raised by them two," Axton said. "Do you ever hear from them now?"

Jack reached for his tea glass. "I hear from my aunt around the holidays. My uncle passed on about a year ago. Everybody was shocked when my mother showed up for the funeral."

Rozlyn was surprised herself. As long as she and Jack had lived together, he had neither seen nor heard from either parent. As far as she knew he hadn't seen them in many years.

"What about your father?" she asked curiously. "That was his brother, wasn't it? Did he show up for the funeral, too?"

His features grim, he shook his head, then swallowed a drink of tea before he answered. "He didn't show. None of us expected him to," he added flatly.

"What about your mama, Jack?" Axton asked. "You must have been glad to see her."

Jack shrugged as he absently pushed the food around on his plate. "We talked. She's doing well and living in Arizona now. I try not to judge her too harshly anymore. Things were—hard when my parents lost the ranch. I couldn't understand why she wanted to leave Rosenberg then. But I was only a boy at the time. I wasn't seeing things as an adult sees them. Besides, she thought my father would be better able to provide for me. That turned out to be a joke, though."

"Hmm, well, I guess there's times all of us are forced into doing things we don't really want to do. I expect that was the way with your mother."

As Axton rose to his feet, he cast a pointed look at Rozlyn. She knew her grandfather was speaking about her and Jack's estrangement. Their separation had hurt the old man, but for a long time Rozlyn had been too lost in her own anger and pain to realize it. She could only hope now that Jack's return wouldn't hurt her or her grandfather again.

Jack said to Axton, "You're not finished eating, are you?"

"Yep, I think I'll go back to the den. I've got a game of solitaire waiting on me."

After her grandfather had left the room, Rozlyn got to her feet and began gathering up the dirty dishes. With quick, methodical movements, she scraped the leftovers into a bowl for the cats who lived at the hay barn.

Jack continued to sit at the table, openly watching Rozlyn's movements. Before supper she'd changed her shirt for a soft, short-sleeved sweater. The swell of her breasts pushed against the scarlet fabric as if to taunt him. Her hair was loose about her shoulders and kept away from her forehead with a wide red ribbon.

He felt a desire to pull her into his arms burning inside him. He didn't know why, he only knew he wanted to bury his hands and face in her hair. He wanted the taste of her mouth on his, her breasts, hips and thighs pressed against his.

Rozlyn was standing at the sink with her back to Jack when she heard the scrape of his chair. Instinctively her head turned toward the sound. She saw that he was now standing. There was a broodiness about his face, a strange darkness in his eyes that made her breath catch in her throat.

"Rozlyn, I think we—"

The telephone rang, interrupting him. Relieved, Rozlyn crossed the few steps to where the instrument hung on the wall and lifted the receiver.

"Hello," she said, then paused as the feminine voice at the other end responded. "Yes, Margaret, he's just fine—in the den playing ole sol. Well—yes, I'll be out most of tomorrow, too, but there's no need for you to check in on him unless you want to." Another pause and then she replied, "All right, I'll tell him you'll be here. Good night, Margaret."

Rozlyn hung the phone on its hook and Jack asked, "Margaret still coming to visit Axton?"

Rozlyn nodded as she went back to her place at the sink. "Faithfully."

Margaret was a widow woman who lived on the outskirts of Llano. While he'd been alive, her husband and Axton had been best of friends. Rozlyn never could figure out why Axton and Margaret had never married. They'd both been widowed for over twenty years and had enjoyed each other's company for that entire time.

Jack watched Rozlyn plunge her hands back into the soapy water. "Rozlyn, earlier I—I meant what I said about helping. It's why I'm here."

She gave him a sidelong glance from her green eyes. "And I meant what I said. I don't need you."

Stepping up beside her, he leaned his hip against the kitchen counter, then raked his fingers through his tousled blond hair. "Look, Rozlyn, I know you're hell-bent on despising me. But right now you'd be damned foolish to turn down my offer."

Turning her head, Rozlyn looked him square in the face. The challenge in his eyes and determined clamp to his jaw sent a wave of hot anger rushing through her.

"And just suppose I did accept your help, Jack?" she said sharply. "What about all the rodeos you'd be missing? Don't tell me you've retired." A shaky laugh escaped her as she turned back to the sink. "For how long? Two weeks, three? Isn't Cheyenne going on about now?''

In spite of her sarcasm, Jack could sense a vulnerability in her that he'd never seen before. It made him want to soothe her in some way, to assure her that he wasn't here to hurt her. Lifting his hand, he softly touched her cheek.

''Whatever you might think, Rozlyn, I didn't choose to make my living rodeoing as a way to hurt or spite you. I thought—after all this time you would realize that.''

Rozlyn didn't say anything. She couldn't. Her knees had gone to jelly the instant Jack had touched her. She didn't want to want him. She didn't want to need him. But a physical ache was warring inside her, begging her to turn and draw him against her.

When she didn't respond, Jack let out a heavy breath. ''As for your question, Cheyenne has already come and gone. I placed second.''

Rozlyn closed her eyes and tried to swallow down the lump that was suddenly clogging her throat. ''That must have won you a thousand or so.''

''No,'' he corrected without conceit, ''it won me several thousand.''

A part of Rozlyn had always been proud of Jack's talent. But that talent had also taken him away from her, and taken away the family and secure home she'd wanted so badly. But Jack had never quite seen it that way.

''That should get you off to a good start this year,''

she murmured. "I'm sure Michael was thrilled about your win."

Her soft, husky voice pulled at everything in Jack. Before he realized it, he was reaching for her with both hands. "Rozlyn, you may not believe me, but I'm sorry about this whole thing with Michael. I know you had hopes that you and he would someday make this place...into the ranch you always wanted it to be."

It was obvious to Rozlyn that Jack still believed it was only a prosperous ranch she'd wanted. He'd never realized it was *him* that she'd wanted more than anything.

Jack's fingers closed over her shoulders, their touch demanding that she look at him. But Rozlyn knew that if she did, he'd see the sadness in her eyes. Twisting her head to one side, she said, "I don't want to talk about Michael. He's made his choice."

Jack's mouth thinned to a disapproving line. "And you're bitter about it," he said flatly. "Have you ever stopped to think how that hurts your brother? The young man I saw down in San Antonio was practically begging me for encouragement."

She forced herself to lift her eyes to his, even though they were shimmering with unshed tears. "I'm not bitter about Michael's choice, Jack. I'm disappointed. I thought—I'd hoped that he cared more for me and the ranch than he did about making a life on the rodeo circuit. I've had to face the fact that he didn't."

In many ways Jack wasn't surprised by what she

was saying. She'd seen things the same way when he'd chosen to continue rodeoing after they were married. "You're talking foolish, Roz. Just because Michael chose a different life from you doesn't mean he no longer loves you."

Rozlyn's gaze focused on Jack's broad chest. It was only inches away from her, and the closeness made her suddenly remember what it had been like to rest her cheek against him. She could almost feel his hand stroking her hair, hear his voice softly reassuring her. But that closeness they'd once shared was gone. It had disappeared the day Jack walked out of her life.

Blinking at the unexpected sting of tears in her eyes, she forced her attention on washing a dirty plate. "You would say that, Jack."

"What is it with you, Roz? Why do you always make it seem as though a person is choosing sides? You did it with me. Now you're doing it with your brother. You—"

He broke off, and Rozlyn's eyes darted up to his face. What had he been going to say? That she'd lost him and now she'd lost Michael? The thought slashed her like a knife. "I what, Jack?" she prompted grittily.

He shook his head. "Nothing. I just wonder why love is something that has to be proved to you."

Hearing Jack say the word *love* sent a charge of emotions rushing through her. Her eyes were simmering with outrage as they fastened pointedly on his face. "How dare you talk to me about love? You don't know the meaning of the word!"

Her accusation made Jack want to shake her. But even more he wanted to kiss her, to shock her, to show her she wasn't the only one who could hurt or feel.

"And I suppose you do?" he drawled, the mocking inflection in his voice daring her to answer.

Incredulous, she stared at him. Jack watched her breasts rise and fall with each deep breath she took. The sight brought images to his mind that made his body burn.

"I've always believed that actions speak louder than words. And your actions never did spell *l-o-v-e*. At least not to me," she said.

Rozlyn had barely spoken before she found herself crushed against Jack's chest. Automatically, she tried to push herself away, but Jack caught hold of her chin, forcing her to remain close to him.

"Don't you dare kiss me!" she whispered shakenly as he lifted her face up to his.

A crooked smile spread slowly across Jack's lips. "Why not? You want action, I'll give you action."

"Jack—" It was all she could manage to say as his face lowered to hers.

"After all, a man has a right to kiss his own wife," he murmured.

As he spoke, his lips moved softly against hers, enticing Rozlyn's senses. She was helpless to resist as his mouth claimed hers. Heat burned its way from her head down to her feet, and without realizing it, she opened her lips to his and lifted her arms to encircle his neck.

Jack was oblivious to everything but the woman in his arms. He moved one hand to her back to press her closer, while sliding the other up to her nape, where he threaded his fingers in her long, silky hair. She tasted soft, sweet and loving.

But she didn't love him, said a voice inside him. She probably never had. He tore his lips away from hers.

Her senses still swimming, Rozlyn opened her eyes to see him dragging in labored breaths. For herself, she wasn't even sure she was breathing.

"Jack—" she began in a dazed voice.

"Is that the kind of action you wanted? Does that tell you anything?" he asked.

Her mouth dropped open at the bitter questions. They seemed almost brutal after the physical reunion they'd just shared. But then she should have known not to put any kind of meaning behind Jack's kiss. Angry at herself for being so gullible, she whirled away from him.

Jack watched her attack the dishes in the sink with a copper scrubber. He hadn't meant to sound so angry with her. Hell, he hadn't even meant to kiss her in the first place. But Rozlyn tempted him in ways that no woman ever had.

Rozlyn could actually feel him standing behind her. She wanted to ignore him. To pretend he wasn't there. But Jack's presence was about as forceful as a Texas tornado and just as impossible to ignore.

"It tells me you don't know any more about love

now than you did two years ago," she muttered fiercely.

Jack folded his arms across his chest as he stood there watching her. "The only kind of love you seem to know about, Rozlyn, is the conditional kind. Even your brother can see that."

Her head whipped around and she fastened a blazing glare on his face. "I didn't ask you to come back here, Mr. Barnett!"

Jack's gray eyes grew dark, almost threatening. "No, you didn't, did you."

Before Rozlyn could respond, he stepped away from her and started out of the kitchen. He was halfway down the hall when her voice called out to him.

"Leaving was always your best event, Jackson! Why don't you do it now?"

His footsteps continued down the hallway. In the kitchen Rozlyn tossed the scrubber back into the soapy water and leaned limply against the cabinet. Tears stung her eyes, and she was shaking so badly her knees threatened to buckle.

Why, she wondered desperately, had her husband decided to come back now? To break her heart all over again?

Almost two hours later, Rozlyn stepped out of the shower and belted herself into a plaid flannel bathrobe that had been given to Axton for a Christmas gift. Since he considered a bathrobe feminine, he'd given it to Rozlyn.

Shivering, she fastened the folds of the fabric tighter around her waist and sat down on the side of the bed. As she pulled a wide-toothed comb through her wet hair, she could hear the wind howling around the corner of the house. Rain was still pelting the windowpanes and she thought about the baby calf. It had come into a harsh world.

"Rozlyn?"

"Yes, Pa, you need something?"

Her grandfather opened the door and stuck his head inside the bedroom. "I just wondered where Jack got off to? I thought he might like a cup of hot chocolate before hitting the sack."

Rozlyn cleared her throat. "I don't know where he is, and I don't particularly care. I asked him to leave."

The old man's face wrinkled into a scowl. "Damn it all, Sis! What the hell is the matter with you?"

She glared at her grandfather. "Pa, don't you curse at me! Jack has no business in this house, or on this ranch."

Axton's reply was to slam the door in his granddaughter's face.

Rozlyn could hear his cane thumping down the hallway. Sighing, she tossed the comb aside and rose from the bed to go stand by the window.

She was still standing there, her mind on her husband, when she heard her grandfather back in the hallway. Without preamble, the old man opened her door.

Rozlyn looked around at him. "What's the matter?" she asked, her voice weary.

"I can't find Jack anywhere in the house—"

Before Axton could say more, Rozlyn hurried past him. In the living room she drew the drapes back just enough to allow her a glimpse of Jack's red truck parked near the yard fence.

Hearing a footstep behind her, she turned to see her grandfather had followed her. "His pickup is still out there," she quickly assured him, "so he has to be around here somewhere."

Axton rubbed his forehead thoughtfully. "Well, he left the den a while ago. Said he had some things to do. I thought he was in the kitchen with you."

Rozlyn shook her head, trying not to think about what had gone on earlier between her and Jack in the kitchen. "Obviously he went outside."

A worried look came over Axton's wrinkled face. "Have you looked outside, Sis? It's freezing out there!"

Sighing, Rozlyn said, "Pa, Jack is a grown man. He knows to get out of the rain."

The older man scowled at her. "Did you ever think two inches in front of you? What if the man went to the barn and one of those damn horses kicked him? You gonna leave him layin' out there to die?"

"Pa, you're getting pretty melodramatic about this," she said, trying her best to be patient. "Even if Jack did go to the barn, he knows his way around a horse better than anyone I know."

Axton snorted, then said in a condescending tone, "Well, you get to bed. I'll go to the barn to find him."

Knowing she was defeated, Rozlyn threw up her hands. "You're not going anywhere."

"I can walk," he assured her.

"I know you can walk. But I'm not about to let you out in this icy rain. I'll go find Jack myself!"

With a nod and a smug grin, the old man turned to leave the room. "That's more like it. I think you'd better go find him right now."

Biting back a curse, Rozlyn turned to leave the room, also. However, something compelled her to look out the window one more time. She gripped the drapes as she leaned closer to the windowpane.

Driven by a cold north wind, rain was slashing horizontally through the night sky. Rozlyn could feel an icy draft seeping around the window casings. It had been cold when she had come in from feeding. The temperature had more than likely dropped several degrees since then.

What was Jack doing? she asked herself. She'd told him to leave. Obviously he hadn't. So where was he? *Could* he have somehow managed to hurt himself? The idea struck a chord of fear in Rozlyn. Turning from the window, she rushed from the room.

The wind was a wet, icy blast as Rozlyn opened the door, then slammed it behind her. The shallow porch on the front of the house did little to shield her from the elements. Quickly she pulled the hood of her rain slicker over her head and struck out for the barn.

From the cab of his pickup, Jack glimpsed the shadowy flicker of Rozlyn's yellow slicker as she dashed in the direction of the barn. What the hell was she doing out in this? he wondered.

Tugging the brim of his hat low over his forehead, he opened the door and stepped out into the freezing rain.

Rozlyn found the barn in complete darkness. Shivering, she pulled a string attached to a single light bulb. The dim light hanging from the rafters flooded over the horse stalls and the sawdust-packed aisle that separated them from a tack room and a large stack of hay.

"Jack? Are you in here?" she called out.

When no answer came, she hurried over to the horse stalls. The gray gelding she'd been doctoring when Jack first arrived this afternoon was now lying down. He blinked drowsily up at Rozlyn as she peered over the gate.

"Go back to sleep, Blue Jeans," she said gently, then stepped over to the next stall where a black horse nickered softly at her.

"What are you doing in here?"

Rozlyn whirled around at the sudden sound of Jack's voice. "Where did you come from?"

It was a relief to see he was all right, and for long moments her eyes drank in everything about him. He was wearing a yellow slicker similar to the one Rozlyn had on. Rainwater and bits of icy sleet slid down its folds and dripped onto his boots.

"I was out in my truck, going through some of my bags when I saw you headed in this direction. I was afraid something was wrong." He took off his Stetson and shook off the water that hadn't yet managed to soak into the expensive felt.

Rozlyn said, "I came down here looking for you. Pa was worried that something had happened to you."

"Pa, huh?" An impish grin spread across his face as he walked slowly toward her. "What about you, Roz? Weren't you just a little worried about me, too?"

She pressed her lips tightly together at his conceited speculation. "It's nothing to joke about, Jack. You could have been lying out here kicked in the head," she said, unaware she was rephrasing her grandfather.

Jack's brows lifted innocently even though the grin remained on his lips. "Who said I was joking?"

Rozlyn deliberately ignored the loaded question. The last thing she wanted to do was give Jack the impression she still cared about him. "I thought— we'd decided you were leaving anyway."

Only inches away from her, Jack rested his arms over the top of the stall gate. "No. *You* may have decided that. I didn't. I've decided I'm staying."

Rozlyn felt herself begin to shiver even harder. Desperately she looked away from him, and back at the horse who was fondly nudging her shoulder. "And where do you get the right to decide about my ranch? My life?"

"I'm still your husband, Rozlyn."

Hearing him say it did strange things to Rozlyn's heart. But she quickly pushed the feelings aside. It would be a foolish mistake to let herself soften toward Jack. "In name only," she reminded him.

"Maybe I'm back here to do something about that," he murmured.

Her head jerked around and her eyes clashed with his gray ones. "What do you mean? I—thought you'd come back to help with the ranch?"

So did Jack. But now that he'd seen Rozlyn again all sorts of things had started running through his head. He was feeling emotions he'd never expected to feel again. But Rozlyn wouldn't understand. He didn't even understand himself.

"I did come back to help," he answered flatly.

Rozlyn expelled a breath of relief even though her expression held plenty of misgivings. "Do you—have a girlfriend?"

The question knocked Jack sideways, though he tried his best not to let her know it. He'd never expected that Rozlyn might wonder about him or his personal life. Did it mean a part of her still cared about him? He couldn't imagine it.

"No. Did you expect me to?"

Rozlyn's gaze slipped guiltily away from him. She shouldn't have asked the question. But it was a question she'd never been able to put entirely from her mind. Even now, the idea of Jack sharing his life with another woman cut at her like a knife.

Shaking her head, she looked back at him. "Forget I asked. It's none of my business." She turned away from him and stepped toward the door. "It's cold out here," she told him. "We'd better get back in before Pa worries himself into a tizzy."

"Rozlyn."

She turned back around to find Jack hovering over her. His eyes were delving into hers, asking questions of their own. Rozlyn drew in a shaky breath, only to find her head reeling with the long-familiar scent of him. It was musky, masculine, erotic. Without warning, something turned over inside of her, and even though she'd just taken a long breath, she felt suffocated.

"What about you, Roz? Do you have a boyfriend?" he asked softly.

She wanted to answer with a mocking laugh. Instead, all she could manage to do was shake her head. "After you, Jack, I haven't really wanted to get out and look for one."

It amazed Jack how relieved he was to hear she wasn't involved with another man. For two years he'd convinced himself he didn't care what she did with her personal life. But now the thought of her touching another man sickened him.

"I half expected Michael to tell me you were seeing another man."

And what would he have done if she had been, Rozlyn silently wondered. Gladly given her a divorce? "Unlike you, Jack, I took our marriage vows seriously."

Even though it was cold inside the barn, she was so close Jack could feel the heat radiating from her body.

He knew how good she would feel if he pushed the slicker aside and drew her against him.

"I tried to take them seriously, Rozlyn. You wouldn't let me. You were more interested in this ranch than you were ever interested in me."

Is that what he really thought? Angrily, Rozlyn tried to push him away, but Jack put his arms around her waist and held her fast against him.

Breathless, she lashed back at him. "That's a lie, Jack, and you know it! I loved you."

His mouth twisted into a mocking sneer. "Yeah, so much so that you forced me to leave."

"I didn't force you," she countered. "You left because you wanted to!"

"You left me no choice. And you know it."

As Rozlyn looked up at his hard face, memories of that day he'd left the ranch flooded her mind. At that time she hadn't known he would stay away so long. Maybe if she had, she would have acted differently. She just didn't know anymore.

"I gave you a choice, Jack, and the choice was me. Obviously, I wasn't what you wanted."

Jack noticed that her voice was growing lower with each word, almost as if it still hurt her to talk of his leaving. The idea stirred something deep within Jack. "I did want you, Rozlyn. I—"

Suddenly Jack was no longer seeing their stormy past. Instead he saw only her upturned face, the dampness of rain on her skin, the dark, wounded look in her eyes, the silent invitation of her parted lips.

"Oh, hell, Rozlyn, why do you do this to me?" he groaned, and bent his head to hers.

The breath stopped in Rozlyn's throat. She knew he was going to kiss her, but she was too mesmerized to do anything about it. All she could think of was the way Jack had once made passionate love to her.

His mouth moved against her cheek, across the bridge of her nose, then to her ear, where he whispered, "Rozlyn, the only thing we ever did right together was making love."

"Oh, Jack—please—" She very nearly panted the words as she fought to hold on to her self-control. She couldn't allow him to touch her like this, not when he'd walked out on her and torn her life apart. But his breath was warm against her face, his lips were so seducing as they moved purposely toward hers.

Jack found it impossible to pull away from her. He sought out her mouth with an urgency that left them both stunned. Rozlyn blindly accepted the invasion of his tongue as it slipped between her teeth and delved into the warm recesses of her mouth.

The onslaught of his passion sent her senses reeling out of control. Unwittingly she groaned and clutched at the front of his slicker.

Without breaking contact with her mouth, Jack moved them both backward until they reached a low stack of loose hay. Rozlyn felt him lowering her down onto it, but still she could not bring herself to break away from his kiss.

Jack pushed aside her wet slicker and discovered

she was wearing nothing under it except a thin flannel robe. He slipped his hand beneath the material, gliding it over her skin until it reached her breast. It was warm and firm against his palm, the nipple budding with arousal.

Moaning with heated response, Rozlyn arched against him, her body silently asking for things it had long been denied. Sensing that her needs matched his, Jack tore his mouth away from hers and impatiently pushed her clothing aside.

Taking her nipple between his teeth, he shifted himself over her. As his mouth drew greedily at her breast, his hands were busy working at the knotted belt at her waist.

By now Rozlyn's whole body was taut with desire. It throbbed and burned until she could think of nothing but having him thrusting into her, making hot, sweet love to her.

She wanted him to make love to her! The realization crashed into her mind like a dash of ice water, and the shock brought common sense rushing back to her drugged mind. As much as she wanted Jack physically, she wasn't about to fall into another mistake. For a week, maybe even two, he'd make glorious love to her, say all the right things to her, and then another rodeo would beckon. He'd leave with a promise that he'd call every day, that he'd be back soon and that he loved her. She'd lived that same scenario for two years. She knew better than to let it happen again.

She shoved her hands against his shoulders. "Let me up, Jack!"

"Roz? What—"

"I said let me up!" She was panicking, desperately needing to put distance between them.

Jack slowly moved away from her and got to his feet. While Rozlyn fumbled with her clothes, he gulped in deep breaths and tried to pull himself together. God, he'd wanted her so much he'd forgotten everything.

Dragging his hands through his hair, he spared her a glance. There was a stark look on her face that cut him to the quick.

"You wanted me," he said, his voice gruff, "but I guess you're going to try to tell me you didn't."

Rozlyn scrambled up from the hay. Without looking at him, she brushed bits of straw from her hair and clothes. "Maybe I did," she muttered. She could hardly deny it when they both knew how wantonly she'd responded to his touch. "But just so you know where I stand, I won't let you make a fool of me again, Jack. You taught me some hard lessons that I'll never forget."

He muttered a curse. "Just because a man kisses you, you think he's trying to make a fool of you? Damn, Roz, but that's twisted! I guess you've buried yourself on this ranch so long you don't even think like a woman anymore."

Rozlyn's face paled at his words. She was afraid Jack was partially right. Until a few moments ago when she'd been in his arms, she'd forgotten what it was like to feel like a flesh-and-blood woman. Yet it wasn't the ranch that had made her that way, she thought. Jack had hurt her so badly she was afraid to feel emotion. Why didn't he realize that?

"If I was truly thinking like a woman," she said quietly, "I wouldn't let you stay."

Jack didn't understand her, but at the moment his mind was so muddled by the need to make love to her, he couldn't think at all. "Does this mean you're going to accept my help?"

She sighed with resignation, then lifted her face to meet his questioning gaze. He couldn't know what he was doing to her. He couldn't know that just looking at his face was making her tremble. "To be honest with you, Jack, I'm hardly in a position to turn down your offer."

The cool, clinical tone of her words mocked the fire still burning inside Jack. Frustrated, he reached for her arm. "Come on, we'd better get back to the house."

He turned out the light, then guided her toward the door. Once there, Rozlyn paused to look up at him. Even though it was impossible to see his face in the darkness, she could easily envision his strong, handsome features. Her voice quivered when she spoke. "One more thing, Jack. You can sleep in Michael's room."

Silent seconds ticked by. Rozlyn was acutely aware of his hand on her arm and the closeness of his body. She still wanted him, but she was determined to make him believe otherwise. Even if it tore her to shreds doing it.

"And maybe I'd rather be back in your room, Rozlyn. Did you ever think about that?" he asked softly.

Heat flared through her at the thought of sharing a bed with him again. To make love with him would be wonderful while it was happening. But she knew how shattering the afterward would be. "To assert your husbandly rights?" she asked tightly.

"If you think I'd want you on those terms, then you never did know me at all," he retorted.

Not waiting for a response from her, he pushed open the huge wooden door that led outside. The icy blast of wind that hit him in the face was for once welcome. It helped to clear his mind. But as they made their way back to the house, Jack wasn't as sure about his heart.

Chapter Three

Rozlyn woke the next morning instinctively knowing she'd overslept. With a groan, she rolled over and checked the clock beside her bed. The arms were straight up and down. Six o'clock.

Quickly she pushed back the cover and sat up on the side of the bed. Two hours sleep had not been enough to rest her weary body. For a moment she held her groggy head in her hands, cursing both Jack and herself for feeling so rotten.

In the past two years, she'd often imagined how she would react if Jack ever showed himself on the ranch again. But none of those images had included falling into his arms as she had last night. Even now her face burned at the memory. She'd kissed him as though she still loved him! Which was crazy. She didn't love Jack. Her love had died a slow, bitter death.

Determined to put the troubling thoughts from her mind, she pushed herself out of bed. There was breakfast to see to and cattle to move. She had little time to waste.

After pulling on blue jeans and a pink turtlenecked sweater, she crossed the hall to the bathroom, where she hurriedly dabbed moisturizer over her face as a protection against the wind. Her long hair, she simply brushed free of tangles and left loose on her shoulders.

Halfway down the hall to the kitchen, Rozlyn could hear voices. The smell of coffee and toast greeted her as she entered the room, telling her Jack had been cooking again.

Both men were seated at the table, and both looked up at the sound of her footsteps.

"Good mornin', Sis," her grandfather greeted. "Get a cup of coffee and join us."

Rozlyn crossed the room, poured herself a mugful of the strong brew, then sipped it carefully as she looked out the kitchen window. Rain was still falling, although this morning it had lessened to a slow drizzle. The day was going to be a nasty one. "We're burning daylight," she told Jack. "Do you have the horses saddled?"

Jack's eyes narrowed as he stared at her in disbelief.

Axton, on the other hand, snorted with outrage. "Is that any way to talk to Jack? He's not your hired hand." The old man tossed a questioning look at Jack, then made a motion toward his granddaughter. "Why don't you take a switch to her? Take some of that uppity stuff out of her.''

Jack shook his head at the old man's suggestion. Even though he knew Axton was joking, he couldn't bear to think of himself, or any man, laying an angry hand on Rozlyn. ''I like a little sass in a woman, Axton. Besides, Rozlyn didn't really mean to sound so bossy. Did you, honey?''

Honey? He'd called her honey just as he used to. Rozlyn wanted to find it offensive, but in truth it melted some of the coldness around her heart.

And with that cold barrier out of the way, memories rushed in. Memories of other mornings, other breakfasts. Jack had always helped her cook the early meal, delegating himself as the sausage-and-bacon fryer. The biscuit making he'd always left to Rozlyn, saying the only kind of dough a man was supposed to handle was the green kind. Rozlyn had often teased him about that. But after he'd left the Broken Spur, there'd been no more teasing, no more shared breakfasts.

An unexpected pain pierced her heart, and she dropped her eyes from his face, down to the coffee cup in her hands. ''No. If I sounded bossy, I didn't mean to. I was merely asking about the horses,'' she said quietly.

Jack's gray eyes sparkled with mischief and he grinned. ''Oh. Well, if you're asking then, no, I haven't saddled. But I've fed. See, I'm half-good.''

Rozlyn looked up at him. It was a surprise to see his grin. A surprise and a pleasure. Without even realizing it, she was smiling back at him. "Sorry, I guess I sounded a bit gung ho, didn't I?"

"If you'd called me 'pilgrim,' I would've thought I was on a cattle drive with John Wayne," he joked, then motioned toward the gas range. "I left a plate of breakfast for you in the oven. Axton and I have already had ours."

He'd cooked breakfast for her? She hadn't expected him to be so thoughtful, and the fact that he had, touched her in spite of her determination to keep a thick wall standing between them. Feeling awkward now, she said with a rush, "I—uh really should go on down to the barn and get the horses ready."

Frowning, Jack got to his feet and fetched the plate from the oven. "Here," he said, placing it on the table in front of her. "Eat. It'll be a long time until lunch. And you can't herd cattle on a cup of coffee."

She looked from him to the plate of food and decided it would be best not to make an issue over her eating the breakfast he'd prepared. "You're right. It will be a long time before we make it back to the ranch to eat lunch."

Taking a seat at the table, she scooted the plate closer to her. It was piled high with scrambled eggs, toast and bacon. The aroma wafting up from the warm food made her stomach growl.

"I overslept this morning," she said. "Usually I'm up earlier than this."

"I know. I remember."

Rozlyn looked up at the soft tone of his response,

and her gaze was caught by his face. It was clean-shaven and his dark blond hair tumbled recklessly over his forehead. He was outrageously handsome, and Rozlyn wondered about the women who'd been attracted to him during his travels. He'd told her he didn't have a girlfriend. Still, she didn't expect he'd lived like a monk these past two years, either.

When her eyes drifted from his hair down to his lips, she was reminded instantly of the previous night. The moment he'd touched her, she had lost every scrap of willpower she possessed. And even later, after she'd gone to bed, she'd lain awake in the darkness, imagining what it would be like to have him lying next to her again. She hadn't been able to quit thinking about him, and even when she had drifted off to sleep, she'd dreamed about him.

The day Jack had left the ranch, she'd sworn to herself that she'd never run after him or beg him to come back. But last night in her dream, she'd been at a rodeo, searching for him, desperately needing to tell him one last time that she still loved him.

The dream had been disturbing, but then so had the way she'd reacted when he'd kissed her so passionately last night. She no longer loved Jack. So why had she dreamed that she did? Why had she turned warm and loving in his arms?

Rozlyn did her best to push the disturbing questions aside for the time being and finish her breakfast. She kissed her grandfather on the cheek before leaving the kitchen to join Jack on the back porch. He was snap-

ping a black duster over his jeans and denim shirt.
Rozlyn tried not to notice how rakishly handsome he
looked, dressed in black from the hat on his head
down to his booted feet.

"You'll need something to turn the rain," he said,
watching Rozlyn slip into a pair of insulated coveralls.

"I have a poncho down at the barn," she told him
as she plopped an old gray felt hat on her head. It was
sweat stained and bent totally out of shape, but at a
time like this, Rozlyn had to consider protection
against the weather instead of fashion. Besides, Jack
ought to know that she didn't have the time or opportunity to dress as a woman.

Cold drizzle fell on Jack and Rozlyn as they made
their way to the barn. When they reached the big double doors, she could hear the injured Blue Jeans paw-
ing at the door of his stall. The sound reminded her
she'd have to ride that damn sorrel that bucked every
time the temperature dipped below fifty.

While Jack went after the saddles and tack, Rozlyn
went to the south side of the barn where a dry lot with
a loafing shed was connected to the larger building.
Two horses and two colts were penned there. She
caught the sorrel and a little black horse she'd bought
off a racehorse trainer living near Brady. The horse
had been on the track a few times, but because he'd
acted a fool in the starting gates, Rozlyn had purchased him for almost nothing. She loved the animal's
sleek lines and speed. Rozlyn would let Jack ride the

black. It would be selfish of her to take him for herself just because her regular horse was out of commission.

She led the two horses back into the barn and tethered them near the tack room. Jack came out carrying a saddle on each shoulder. He added them to the pile of pads and blankets already lying to one side.

"Put your saddle on the black, Jack," Rozlyn suggested, trying her best to sound casual. "He's green, but he's nice."

Jack eyed the horse from both sides, then ran his hands expertly over his back and hips, then down each leg. "He looks racy," he commented.

"He should," Rozlyn answered proudly. "He was sired by Rocket Wrangler. Isn't he beautiful?"

With mild surprise, Jack looked from the horse over to Rozlyn. For the first time since he'd arrived yesterday, there was a bright, eager look on her face. It softened her eyes and the full lines of her mouth, reminding Jack irresistibly of the happy young woman he'd first fallen in love with.

Actually, it had been a horse, a beautiful paint horse named Mighty Warrior, that had caused Jack and Rozlyn to meet. Both of them had been attending a horse sale in San Antonio and both had unknowingly chosen to bid on the same horse. When Jack had spotted Rozlyn across the auction ring discreetly lifting her finger at the auctioneer, he'd taken one long look at her and backed off the bidding.

"I can see you're already attached to him," Jack

spoke up. "But what about Mighty Warrior? He's a better cow horse than even Blue Jeans."

A shadow crossed Rozlyn's face as she bent down to pick up a currycomb. "I sold him," she murmured.

Jack was stunned. "Sold him! Lord, I can't believe that. You loved that horse. Besides that, you needed him."

Yes, Rozlyn had needed the horse, but she'd needed the money even more. However, she wasn't going to air her financial problems to Jack. Even though he'd chosen to leave her, it wasn't her husband's fault that Axton had required special medical attention, or that the drought last fall had taken a toll on the cattle as they headed into winter. She'd lost several cow-and-calf pairs, and the loss had cut deeply into the ranch's profits. "I had a chance to make some money on him, so I did."

"I see," he said, but frankly he didn't. He knew Rozlyn had loved the horse. But then, of course, she'd loved Jack, too. Or so she'd once said, a long time ago. Yet she'd disposed of both of them. The idea hurt. He couldn't help remembering the easy way his parents had disposed of him, too.

Careful to avoid Jack's face, Rozlyn raked the currycomb over the sorrel's thick, damp coat. There was no doubt that, like her, Jack was remembering the day she'd purchased Mighty Warrior.

He'd come up to her just as Rozlyn had been loading the gelding into a trailer. When he'd introduced himself and offered her a five-hundred-dollar profit for the paint, she'd decided then and there that Jackson Barnett was not only bold, but was also a man who knew and appreciated good horseflesh.

Rozlyn had turned down his offer for the horse, however, she'd been unable to resist his offer for dinner that night. He'd been devastatingly handsome, and Rozlyn, who'd been only twenty, and innocent for her age, had found his earthy sensuality overpowering.

Yet it hadn't been just the physical part of their relationship that Rozlyn had fallen in love with. Complex, exciting and a complete maverick, Jack had been the exact opposite of Rozlyn, who'd always lived life with careful, single-minded determination. In some strange, inexplicable way, it had been that very difference that had drawn her to him.

And he was still that same complex man, she thought. Only he was no longer *her* man.

"Well, Jack," she said, clearing her husky voice as she attempted to shake away her memories. "You know Mighty Warrior was nine when I bought him. So he was beginning to get on in years."

She didn't know if she was trying to justify her actions to Jack or herself. She'd grieved for days over selling the horse. She'd believed then it was simply because she'd had to part with a favorite animal, but now she wondered if she'd hated parting with the horse because it had somehow symbolized the love she and Jack shared.

"Some horses are just coming into themselves when

they reach fourteen. I'm sure he would have had many good years left,'' Jack reasoned.

There was no accusation in his statement. Rozlyn was grateful for that much, at least. Parting with Mighty Warrior was a painful reminder to her of both her broken marriage and the ranch's financial problem. She didn't want to dwell on either now.

Jack continued to brush down the black horse, but he kept glancing over at Rozlyn. Her back was to him and he wished she would turn around and face him. For some reason it was important to him to know what she was thinking and feeling. Was she, like him, remembering back to happier times when they'd loved each other?

Rain continued to fall as the two of them rode their horses toward the west pasture. Rozlyn had pulled a weatherproof poncho over her coveralls to keep from getting soaked. With each hard gust of cold wind, the material billowed and snapped against the sorrel's sides, sending the horse into a nervous prance.

By the time they reached the cattle, Rozlyn was exhausted from seesawing on the bridle reins in order to control the animal. The black, under Jack's special touch, was behaving like a well-broken cow pony.

Groaning inwardly, she pulled the sorrel to a halt and reached up to wipe the rain from her face. Jack stopped a foot or two away from her, his narrowed eyes going over her and her horse.

"Why did you ride that idiot?"

Frustration made her glare at him. "Because this idiot, as you call him—his name's Buster, incidentally—was all I had. Blue Jeans got his foot caught in barbed wire. That's why I have him stalled."

"You could have ridden this black. I couldn't ask for a nicer pony."

"That's why I gave him to you," she told him, her voice softening. "I wanted you to have him."

He'd learned long ago that Rozlyn could be a mystery. It both surprised and bewildered him that she would give him the better horse. Jack could ride anything with four legs, so he knew she hadn't done it out of concern for his safety. Did that mean she'd done it out of kindness?

"But that doesn't mean he won't buck you off in the next thirty minutes," she added, not wanting him to get the wrong idea about her generosity.

"Humph," he grunted, his expression a bit arrogant. "This horse couldn't shake me loose if he bucked all the way back to the ranch."

"Not at all conceited, are we, Jack?" Rozlyn asked, her voice more teasing than anything.

Laughing, Jack reached up and tugged at the brim of his hat. Rain poured in a stream off the black felt and Rozlyn knew the hat would never be the same again. He'd probably given an arm and leg for it. To play true to the part of being a cowboy, he'd say. The thought brought an even deeper smile to Rozlyn's lips.

"You find something funny about being cold and wet?" he asked.

Feeling a sudden lift in her spirits, she laughed. "It does me good to see you working like us common folks, Jack."

The corner of his mouth lifted. "I am common folks. And I do work, Roz. Whatever you might think, riding a rank bull *is* work."

Jack common? The idea was ludicrous. Even if he were just a rancher instead of a rodeo champion, he would never be common.

Rozlyn waved her arm out over the ragged landscape dotted with mesquite, prickly pear and choya. "But there's no cheering crowds around here, Jack," she pointed out. "No big dollars."

"Man does not live on glory alone, Roz." It had been something he'd learned this past two years during his quest to reach the top. Glory was good for the ego. Certainly it had been strong enough to keep pushing him down the road, but it hadn't made him happy. In spite of his success, he felt empty inside.

But maybe that was the way it was meant to be for Jack Barnett, he thought. Surely it hadn't been in God's plan for him to have a real mother and father, a proper home. Rozlyn had wanted Jack to make the Broken Spur his proper home, his permanent home. But his early life had proved to him that things didn't always last, and the best way to avoid the pain of losing them was to never have them in the first place.

But Jack had wanted Rozlyn so badly, loved her so deeply he'd married her anyhow. Somehow, he'd sworn, he would make it last. He knew the mistakes his mother and father had made, and he was bound and determined not to let the same thing happen to him and Rozlyn.

It was one of the reasons Jack hadn't wanted to make the Broken Spur their permanent home. His job was rodeoing, a job that kept him on the road traveling from one town to the next. After seeing what his parents had gone through, that sort of rolling-stone life seemed much more sensible to him than struggling over a piece of land with a herd of cows on it.

Ironically, the very thing Jack set out to avoid, in hopes of making their marriage last, had ultimately brought about its end.

"I believe you could live on glory alone, Jack. You never seemed to really need anything else."

Rozlyn's words broke into his thoughts. He turned his eyes to her. How young and vulnerable she looked, hunched over the saddle horn, the cold rain dripping from her battered hat. In that moment he felt an overwhelming need to protect her, to make things better for her.

"Maybe you never really knew me, Roz. And maybe I didn't know myself," he added in afterthought, a wry twist to his lips.

Buster shifted restlessly beneath Rozlyn, and she reached to stroke a soothing hand down his neck. Jack's admission had taken her by surprise. Was he finally admitting that perhaps he'd been partly to blame for their broken marriage? The idea disturbed her and she felt an urgent need to get away from the personal tone their conversation had taken.

Reining Buster around, she motioned toward the cattle in the near distance. "How are we going to handle moving the herd?"

While Jack took a quick survey of the animals and the surrounding terrain, Rozlyn was content to remain silent, huddled beneath the poncho as the cold wind sliced across the flat pasture land.

After a moment Jack said, "Right now, just stay out to the right of them while I get them tightened together. Hopefully, the cold wind will make them want to stay bunched."

Nodding, she urged her horse away from him. Fifty yards away she guided the animal down a shallow ravine, then stopped and waited until Jack had the herd moving. It didn't take much effort, just a yelp or two and the slap of Jack's lariat against his thigh.

Rozlyn wasn't surprised at the cattle's lack of resistance. They were cold and hungry, and probably thought anywhere would be better than this barren pasture they were now foraging.

The next hour they urged the cattle along at a slow pace back over the route Jack and Rozlyn had taken earlier. The journey moved the cattle over barren flats, around and through thick mesquite, down and across wide arroyos that had become wet and boggy from the overnight rains.

Rozlyn did her best to keep the sorrel in hand and watch for any strays that cared to venture away from the group. The freezing wind had caused her feet and hands to go numb. As for her face, she wasn't sure it was there anymore.

Yet, she was finding Jack's presence more of a distraction than the bitter weather. She could deal with numb feet and fingers, but it was a different matter when it came to dealing with a man who had once been her lover.

A hundred yards ahead of the herd, a barbed-wire fence ran north and south across the horizon. Before they reached it, Jack turned the cattle in a southerly direction toward a metal gate that would open onto another eighty-acre section of pasture.

Rozlyn was relieved their trek was nearly over. She wanted to get back to the ranch where she could get off the temperamental horse she was riding and warm her numb body.

While Jack dismounted to open the gate, Rozlyn hovered at the edge of bawling animals. As soon as the metal barrier swung wide, the cattle began to bolt through the opening, barely giving Jack time to climb the fence and get out of their path. At the back of the pack three steers, apparently frightened by the small stampede, broke away and began running down a narrow gully off to Rozlyn's right.

Digging her heels into Buster's side, she quickly went after the strays, hoping to head them off before they climbed out of the gully.

"Ho, cattle!" she yelled, waving her arms at the runaway steers.

Quickly glancing ahead, Rozlyn could see the ground breaking away as the gully narrowed and cut upward into higher ground. She didn't have to touch the sorrel's reins to stop him. Buster jabbed his front feet into the ground in such a sudden halt that Rozlyn was thrown against the saddle horn with a force that nearly winded her.

"Damn horse!" she muttered. Reining the horse away from the wide gap in the ground, she urged him into a flying gallop to where the cut in the ground was narrow enough to jump.

"Rozlyn, let them go!"

She could hear Jack's voice calling to her, but she ignored him. She'd never rest if the three steers got away.

As Rozlyn neared the more narrow part of the gully, the horse balked again. This time Rozlyn swatted his hindquarters with her hat. But instead of jumping the gully, the horse ducked his head and broke into a hard buck.

Her mind had been so set on catching the steers, she'd forgotten that Buster couldn't be trusted. Frantically she attempted to jerk up the reins, but the horse had already taken control. Before Rozlyn knew what was happening, she was hurtling over his head and straight toward the gully.

Jack, who'd witnessed the whole thing from his position on the fence, was on the ground and running as Rozlyn landed in a crumpled heap in the bottom of the narrow wash.

"God Almighty!" he muttered as he scrambled down the steep, muddy embankment.

Rozlyn groaned as he touched her shoulder. "Jack?"

Her voice was faint. The dark crescents of lashes on her cheeks fluttered but remained closed.

"Roz, where does it hurt?" he asked, feeling her arms and legs gently.

"I'm—just winded," she finally managed to get out between ragged spurts of breath. She struggled to push herself up. "I need—to sit up."

Immediately Jack shifted his arm beneath her shoulder and lifted her to a sitting position. "Don't try to hurry it," he warned, "just breathe slowly."

As the oxygen filled her lungs, Rozlyn felt her strength returning. She opened her eyes to see Jack's face hovering anxiously over hers. Her heart nearly stopped at the gentle, tender way he was holding her against him. It almost made her believe she was still precious to him.

"I'm really all right now, Jack," she said more firmly.

"Are you sure? You took a hard spill." He lifted and brushed the hair away from her face. She still looked pale to him and the pulse at the base of her throat was a rapid flutter. He didn't want her to move too soon and risk the chance of her fainting. And, oddly enough, he didn't want to quit holding her. She'd scared him badly. So badly that what he really wanted to do was crush her to him and never let go.

"It was a foolish spill," she muttered. "That damn Buster has a BB-sized brain!"

Her anger at the horse was bringing a flush of color back to her cheeks. Jack was relieved to see it. "I suppose that's why he's halfway back to the ranch by now," he said wryly.

"What? Halfway back—" Rozlyn jerked her head swiftly around in search of the sorrel horse. Not only did she not see him, but the sudden movement sent her head spinning. "Oh—my," she groaned faintly.

Vaguely she felt Jack press her head back against his shoulder. She closed her eyes and waited for the wave of dizziness to pass. It felt too good here in his arms, she thought drowsily. A few more moments and she might not want to leave them.

"Stay still for a minute or two," he ordered as Rozlyn stirred against him. "And while you're at it, forget about the damn horse! We'll ride the black back to the ranch."

Ride double? Just the idea of being in such close contact with Jack was enough to clear her foggy head. Drawing on all the strength she could muster, Rozlyn pushed away from him and stood on her feet.

At first she teetered unsteadily, and Jack reached out for her arm to help support her.

"What about the steers?" she asked, unaware of just how weak her voice still sounded to him. "Did they get away, too?"

Jack shook his head. "After Buster bucked you off,

they decided to turn and run back to the rest of the herd.''

Rozlyn attempted a laugh as she wiped a shaky hand across her forehead. "So it looks like I landed on my head for nothing."

Jack's mouth twisted into a rueful grin. "It looks that way." Actually, in that moment when he'd seen her flying headfirst into the arroyo, he was certain his heart had stopped beating. He'd seen many of his rodeo buddies get trampled, kicked and crushed, but none of those sights had terrified him as much as the fall Rozlyn had just taken. The fear of finding her bleeding or broken had left his hands shaking, his heart pounding. He still wasn't quite over it.

Jack reached for Rozlyn's hat, then crammed it back onto her head. "If you're all right, let's get out of here," he said, his voice gruff from the unexpected emotions threatening to swamp him.

Rozlyn nodded, and Jack took her by the hand to lead her up the side of the steep arroyo. The ground was slippery, and she lost her footing once, but Jack's hold on her arm prevented her from falling.

"The black has probably never been ridden double," she told him once they were back onto higher, flatter ground. "You're going to get me bucked off twice in one day."

"I don't really see that we have much of a choice in the matter," Jack told her. "Both of us have to ride, or one of us will have to walk. And it's too far, wet, and cold for that."

He was right, but that didn't make her like the idea any better. Riding double with Jack would virtually put her in his arms, and that was far too close for Rozlyn's peace of mind.

Jack had left his mount tethered next to the gate where the cattle had passed through. While he went after it, Rozlyn wiped at the mud smeared across her poncho and the legs of her coveralls.

Now that her head was clearing from the fall, she was feeling like an idiot for allowing the horse to throw her. She'd always wanted Jack to think she was efficient and capable at anything she went to do. Now there was no telling what he was thinking. Especially after she'd given him that speech yesterday of how she could take care of herself and the ranch without any help.

"Does this horse have a name?" he asked as he led the animal to a stop just a few feet away from her. "It's insulting to him to keep calling him by his color."

"His name is 'A Real Rocket,'" Rozlyn told him as she rubbed her hands up and down her backside. She looked up to catch the faint grin on Jack's face. "I forgot. You're a man who knows all about being bucked off. Being bruised and sore."

He laughed softly. "It always bruised my ego more than it did anything else," he assured her, then motioned for her to come there. "See if you can get on. We'll find out for ourselves if he's A Real Rocket."

Reluctant to begin the dreaded journey back, Rozlyn

hesitated. "Maybe you should ride up front and I'll sit behind the saddle," she suggested. At least that way she could hold on to the saddle and not have to be so close to him.

"No. You'll forget and get your heels in his flanks, then we'll both be landing on our heads."

It was on the tip of Rozlyn's tongue to remind him that she knew how to ride a horse. But that would more than likely produce a howl of laughter from him. And considering her performance a few minutes ago, she couldn't very well blame him.

After Rozlyn had settled herself into the saddle, Jack gave her the reins and positioned his left hand on the swell of the saddle. Without bothering to use the stirrup for a toehold, he made one sweeping leap that landed him squarely on the horse's hindquarters behind Rozlyn.

The unaccustomed weight caused the animal to dance sideways. Rozlyn gathered the reins tighter and soothed him with her voice and the stroke of her hand. Jack scooted up close behind Rozlyn, then reached around her waist.

"Here, give me the reins," he told her.

Rozlyn's breath released in jerky spasms as she handed the braided nylon over to Jack's strong, capable hand. He was so close his chest was rubbing her back, his thighs were pressed closely against the backs of hers. In spite of the cold wind, heat washed through her.

"Now you think I can't ride," she said, blurting out

anything to get her mind off what his closeness was doing to her.

"No. I think you can't pick your mounts."

She drew in another long breath of cold, damp air. "Buster is as green as grass. He'll be a good cow horse once I have time to train him. Besides, I traded that old high-back saddle with the iron stirrups to Lester Daly for him."

"Well, Lester certainly got the better end of the deal. You could have probably sold that saddle to a museum for a good price. Instead you got something that might break your neck."

The horse's walk was now smoothing out as he grew accustomed to the weight of his two riders. Normally the steady rhythm would have relaxed Rozlyn, but not now. Each movement had Jack's legs pushing and rubbing against hers. The contact sent jolts of sizzling heat rushing through her, making it an effort to keep her mind on his words instead of his body.

She drew in a much-needed breath, then replied, "Buster will come along, once I have time to work with him."

Jack's arm suddenly pressed against her side as he reined the horse around a boggy patch of ground. She closed her eyes and wondered how just his touch could still have the power to affect her.

"If I had anything to say about it," he went on speaking of the unruly horse, "he'd leave this ranch."

Anger at his arrogance and her own weakness made

her voice come out sharp. "But you don't have anything to say about it, Jack."

Jack thought of reminding her once again that he was still legally her husband, but decided against it. What good would it do? he asked himself. Rozlyn knew, just as well as he, that according to a piece of paper they were still married. Yet in spite of that legal document, she didn't consider him her husband anymore. So why was he now thinking of her as his wife?

By the time they'd ridden ten minutes, the drizzle stopped, but the wind picked up in strength, sending the low-hanging clouds scudding quickly across the gray sky. Before Rozlyn could catch herself, she was hunching against the warmth and shelter of Jack's body.

Realizing she was cold, Jack tried to shield her from the wind as much as possible. But even he found himself shivering from the bone-chilling dampness. It made him wonder where she found the strength to go on working this place. Dirty, tiring, never-ending tasks had to be done over and over, day in, day out to keep a ranch going. And even if a person did manage to have a good calf crop, it didn't mean the price of beef would remain stable. Most women would never want the kind of life Rozlyn had, and Jack had never been able to figure out why she wanted it. Maybe if he had, they would still be living together.

"Are you sure that fall didn't twist or sprain something?" he asked as the horse lumbered along at an easy walk.

Until his voice had broken the silence, Rozlyn had been lost in time. The circle of his arms around her, the warmth of his breath against the back of her neck had slowly seduced her, tugging her mind back to when they'd been together.

She shook her head in hopes of scattering the bittersweet memories from her thoughts. "I don't think so."

The movement of her head drew Jack's eyes to the fall of hair lying against her back. It was damp from the rain, making the color opaque and rather nondescript, but Jack knew that once it dried, the curls would take on a fiery life of their own.

There had been times in the past when Rozlyn had sat between his legs while he'd brushed her hair until it snapped and crackled beneath his hands. The memory had Jack reaching up and rolling a curl between his fingers.

Even though his touch was feather light, Rozlyn was acutely aware of his fingers in her hair. She kept her eyes straight ahead and told herself not to remember how good it used to be between them. She told herself to ignore the quiver of anticipation in her stomach.

"I'll be fine once I get home, Jack," she added, though she wasn't really sure who she was trying to reassure. Him, or herself.

Home. It was all she'd ever needed or wanted, he realized. With a rueful twist on his mouth, Jack dropped the curl he'd wrapped around his finger and jammed his hand back into the pocket of his duster.

In front of him, Rozlyn released a long, tense breath. For one split second, she'd thought he was going to turn her around and kiss her. Heaven help her, she'd more than thought it, she'd wanted it!

What was happening to her? She shouldn't be wanting Jack. He was irresponsible and selfish. Time after time he'd put his wants and needs before hers. Still, she couldn't forget the fear she'd seen in his eyes when he'd found her at the bottom of the arroyo. She couldn't forget the tenderness in his hands as he'd touched her face and brushed the hair from her eyes. Even more, she couldn't forget the sweet fire that rushed through her veins whenever he kissed her.

But she had to forget. If she didn't, she was going to wind up with her heart stepped on all over again.

"I don't care what you say, old man, I'm not fixing you any ham and red-eye gravy. Just what would Roz think if she saw you eating such stuff?"

Margaret's voice carried from the kitchen and onto the back porch where Rozlyn and Jack were shedding their wet outer clothing.

As the two of them entered the warm kitchen, Axton was grumbling. "I've managed to eat without any help for more than eighty years. Now you tell me I need my granddaughter to show me how to do it?"

"Margaret is right," Rozlyn spoke up. "You're not

about to eat ham floating on a plate of grease. Just what do you think that would do to your arteries?''

The older woman, standing at the kitchen sink, turned with a look of relief on her broad, wrinkled face. "Thank goodness—" she broke off abruptly as she spotted Jack entering the room behind Rozlyn. Surprise and joy swept across her face.

"My Lord, Jack! Is that you?"

Jack smiled as the heavyset woman rushed toward him.

"Hello, Margaret. How are you?"

"Land sakes, it is you!" she exclaimed, flinging her arms around him and crushing him to her ample bosom. "It's so good to see you, boy."

Jack laughed as Margaret let go of him, only to grab his chin. Turning it one way and then the other, she closely inspected his face. "Just as handsome as ever! I see those bulls haven't knocked out any of those pretty white teeth."

In spite of his thirty-one years, Jack felt a blush spread across his face. "No. These are all mine."

Her features all smiles, Margaret patted his shoulders.

Rozlyn quietly edged away from them and moved to the other side of the room. Seeing Jack and Margaret meeting again after so long was making her feel ridiculously sentimental.

Jack was also affected, warmed by Margaret's greeting. He pressed a kiss on the older woman's cheek and said, "You're looking mighty pretty, Margaret. How do you do it?"

She yelped with laughter, then waved her hand at him as she went back to her place at the kitchen sink. "I can see you're still a flatterer, too, Jackson." She looked over her shoulder at Axton. "You didn't tell me Jack had come back," she said accusingly.

"I hadn't had time, woman. You've been flapping your jaws ever since you walked in the door this morning."

Margaret rolled her eyes impatiently at the old man, then turned to where Rozlyn was filling two mugs with coffee. The older woman's face was full of questions. Rozlyn knew that Margaret would grab the first chance she got to question her about Jack.

"Have you fixed anything for lunch yet, Margaret?"

"Sure have. Chicken and noodles, and there's hot bread fixing to come out of the oven."

"I can already smell it," Jack said, sniffing.

"Well, I'm glad someone around here appreciates my cooking," she said with a pointed look at Axton.

"Humph," he snorted. "I've ate so much chicken that I'm just about ready to lay an egg. A man wants good pork once in a while." Axton turned his attention to Jack, who was removing his hat and hanging it on a peg on the wall. "Son, I want you to go over to the livestock sale at Brady tomorrow and buy me a hog."

"Pa! Jack isn't going to do any such thing!" Rozlyn

declared. "You'd just make a pet out of the thing anyway."

"Well, that might be all right. At least I'd have one friend around here," Axton snorted.

Rozlyn crossed the room to Jack and offered him the coffee. He took it with a look of mild surprise.

"Thank you, Roz," he said in a low voice.

"You're welcome," she responded, her eyes briefly meeting his.

She knew he was probably wondering why she'd done the small kindness for him. In all honesty, Rozlyn was wondering, too. She kept telling herself it was for the concern he'd shown her when she'd fallen, but there was also a tiny part of her that wanted to show Jack she hadn't turned into a complete shrew.

Quickly she moved away from him and went to help Margaret dish up the lunch she'd prepared. Behind her, Jack took a seat beside her grandfather.

"You're forgetting I'm here now, Axton. You've got me for an ally."

The old man gave him a toothless grin. "Yeah, that's right, son. And you know it makes me happy. For the first time in a long time I woke up this morning happy 'cause I knew you was back home with us."

Back home, Jack thought. Funny how right that felt to him.

As if they had a will of their own, his eyes moved to his wife. She was standing on tiptoe, pulling plates down from the cabinet. Her pink sweater had ridden above the waistband of her jeans, exposing a strip of smooth, white skin.

Jack realized he wanted to go to her, put his arms around her waist and fit his body up against hers. Just as he had when they'd loved each other, when it had been a natural thing to touch her as his wife.

"Well, I'm glad I've come back, too, Axton," Jack said, and realized he *was* happy, happier than he'd been in ages.

"This is the best news I've had in years!" Margaret exclaimed as she turned and placed a pot of stewed chicken and noodles in the middle of the table. "I want to hear all about your travels. How long you plan on staying, Jack?"

Jack felt, more than saw, three pairs of eyes turn on him. But it was Rozlyn's questioning eyes that worried him the most. How long did she want him to stay, he wondered. How long did *he* want to stay?

"I—uh—"

"Well, you're not going to be leaving before tomorrow night, are you?" Margaret pressed.

Relieved that Margaret had given him a question he could answer, he looked up at the older woman and grinned. "No. I'll still be here. Why do you ask?"

"Oh, you just might want to come to my birthday party tomorrow night," she said happily.

Rozlyn's coffee cup stopped midway to her lips. She'd forgotten all about Margaret's party. True, it had been all the woman had talked about for the past two weeks, but Jack's return had pushed everything but him from Rozlyn's mind.

"I just might," Jack said. "Thanks for asking me."

Jack had always been more of a socializer than she was, Rozlyn thought. He used to love to dance, and he could strike up a conversation with anyone, anywhere. Whereas Rozlyn had always been a stay-at-home, no-nonsense person. It wasn't that she disliked people or having fun. There'd been many nights after her parents had died that she'd longed to be able to go out to dances and parties like her other teenage friends.

But there'd always been work to do—running a household, doing the ranch chores, and seeing after her younger brother and elderly grandfather's needs. During those first months without her parents, the crush of burden on Rozlyn's shoulders had been almost unbearable. Until little by little, as the years fell behind her, she'd matured and learned how to carry the weight of responsibility.

Yes, she'd learned all about holding the ranch and her family together. But she hadn't learned about having fun.

Chapter Four

Lunch passed with Margaret doing most of the talking. Jack listened patiently as she tried to catch him up on all the Llano happenings of the past two years. He responded in all the right places, but the bigger part of him was focused on Rozlyn. She seemed unusually drawn and quiet. And it bothered Jack to see her that way. He wished he could see her smiling, laughing, a sparkle in her green eyes. In fact, he found himself wishing it more and more.

Margaret was still firing questions at Jack when Rozlyn excused herself and slipped down the hallway to the bathroom.

She was shaking two aspirin into her palm when she heard a light footstep behind her.

"Are you all right, Rozlyn?"

She'd known it was Jack even before he spoke. It

was as if her body had a highly sensitive radar whenever he was near.

"Yes. I just have a little ache in my left shoulder. It's nothing." Actually it had started as a little ache on the ride back to the ranch. Now it had grown into a continuous throb, but she wasn't going to tell Jack that. She didn't want his sympathy.

The next thing Rozlyn knew, his hands were on her shoulder, kneading the soft flesh around it. "Maybe you should be X-rayed," he suggested.

Jack's hands sent a shaft of desire ripping through her. She couldn't prevent a soft gasp from passing her parted lips.

Jack instantly mistook the sound she made for pain. Keenly, he examined her face, which was flushed with heat. "Did I hurt you?"

Not physically, she thought. Not ever physically. Her heart began to beat faster and faster. "No, it's— I'm fine, Jack. There's no need to worry about me."

She quickly averted her face from his all-too-seeing eyes. Jack's fingers tightened on her shoulder. "You don't have to pretend with me, Roz. When you left the table, I saw your face. Something's wrong."

For some reason his soft-spoken concern upset her far more than anything he'd said to her. It made her remember how tenderly he used to love her, made her wonder if it could ever be that way again. But that was futile, dangerous thinking. Jack was a man who would ultimately hurt her again. He hadn't changed. He wouldn't change.

Grimacing, she turned back to the sink and filled a glass with water. "Okay, I hurt," she said crossly, then tossed the aspirin into the back of her throat. She washed them down with the water before adding, "Is that what you wanted? A confession from me?"

No, he thought, that wasn't what he wanted. Before he could stop himself, he had yanked her into his arms and brought his mouth savagely down on hers.

At first Rozlyn was too stunned to resist, then the shock of his mouth on hers plunged her into a panic. She couldn't give in to him! She couldn't allow him to melt her resistance with just a kiss!

Struggling, she tried to wedge her arms between them. Jack lifted his mouth, just enough to speak. "You asked me what I wanted, Rozlyn. I'm answering your question."

"No! You don't want—"

His mouth closed over hers once again, cutting off her protest. Rozlyn was suddenly torn between the need to turn to him and the need to pull herself away. Desperately she tried to turn her face to one side.

Jack's fingers closed around her chin and held it fast. "Don't fight me, Roz," he pleaded hoarsely. "Kiss me. Now. Like you used to."

The hungry sound in his voice and the warmth of his breath on her face sent shivers of longing down her spine. With a fatalistic moan, she pressed closer to him. Jack took her mouth while nudging the door shut with the toe of his boot.

Rozlyn felt herself going under as his tongue

slipped into her mouth, teasing her, tasting her with a rhythm that matched the pagan throb between her thighs.

"Jack—" she breathed, partly in protest, partly as a plea.

Jack barely heard her speak his name. Desire was swiftly taking control of his mind as his mouth fed at hers. With his fingers, he worshiped her face, her throat, then moved urgently downward to where her breast thrust against the soft fabric of her sweater.

Rozlyn felt utterly lost as his hands slipped beneath her sweater and cupped around each breast. Wedged against his chest, her fingers opened and closed convulsively, then as if in surrender slid up to his neck.

Groaning deep in his throat, Jack thrust his hips forward, pressing his urgent need against Rozlyn's belly. It made her instantly aware of his arousal, and the fierce need to appease both him and herself was suddenly gripping her body and mind.

Shifting, she moved her hips against his. Jack's hands deserted her breasts to clutch her rounded bottom. Desperately, he crushed her closer, grinding into her with a need that left Rozlyn gasping aloud and gripping his shoulders.

"Rozlyn, oh, Rozlyn—" he groaned against her throat. "I want you! Do you know how much?"

"Yes."

It was all she could say. It was all she wanted to say. She was on fire for him. All she could think about was having him inside her, taking her to a place that only he could take her.

She writhed against him and called out his name. "Jack! I want—you!"

Hearing her say it not only inflamed his senses, it touched something in his heart. "Oh, Rozlyn, we—were so good like this. No matter what—it was good."

She couldn't deny his hoarsely whispered words, because they were true. She couldn't deny him her body, either. Not when she wanted his just as badly.

Her hands went to his shirt and quickly began to tear apart the pearl snaps. When the material opened beneath her hands, she leaned forward and pressed her lips to his heated skin. Jack shivered in response and meshed his fingers in long hair.

"I don't know where those two got off to. Maybe they went back down to the barn," said Axton just outside the door.

"Well, this cobbler is hot, and I know how Rozlyn likes peach cobbler," Margaret replied.

The sudden interruption acted like a sheet of cold rain on Rozlyn and Jack. They both went stock-still, then Rozlyn abruptly jerked away from him.

Dear God, what was she doing? It was the middle of the day. Margaret and her grandfather were just down the hall. And she'd been close to making love to Jack on the bathroom floor!

"Roz, don't be—"

"How did I let you do this to me?" she hissed

under her breath as she frantically tried to put her clothes in order.

"Let me?" he echoed, his low voice still hoarse with desire. "You weren't letting me. You were asking for it."

He was right. She didn't understand it. She thought she hated him, but the more he touched her, the more she wanted him.

"Maybe I was," she mumbled. "But that doesn't make it right."

Jack, who'd been snapping his shirt back together, forgot the task and reached out to grasp her shoulders. "It felt right to me, and it felt right to you! Why are you trying to deny it?"

Sparks flared in her green eyes as she looked up and into his face. "Because I know this is going to take us nowhere! Sex would fix nothing between us."

The rigid lines on his face suddenly relaxed, and his voice grew soft. "Would you like for it to be fixed, Rozlyn?"

The question stunned her. For long seconds she merely stared at him. What did he mean? Surely he wasn't asking if they should get back together. No, it was too much to comprehend. Especially when her body was still aching for his.

"I can't answer that, Jack. Not now." She pushed around him and reached for the door. "I—we'd better get out of here before Pa or Margaret finds us."

For the rest of the day, Rozlyn could think of nothing but Jack's question. Did some part of her want them to get back together? Those few minutes she'd spent in his arms had been like heaven. But she knew heaven with Jack wasn't a lasting one.

The two of them worked until dark, hauling hay and feed out to the cattle. After what had taken place in the bathroom, Rozlyn expected an awkward hostility from Jack. But after a few minutes, it was obvious from his easy attitude that he was going to put aside their differences. At least while they were working.

Rozlyn was grateful for that much, at least. Still she was constantly aware of him as they worked side by side, unloading the hay and spreading feed pellets out for the hungry cattle.

Jack was a hard worker. Rozlyn had always known he could accomplish what it usually took two normal men to do. She could certainly never accuse him of being shiftless. Those times he'd been at home, he'd always put all of himself into helping Rozlyn on the ranch. But the longer they were married, those times he'd remained at home had grown further and further apart.

Rozlyn had seen it happening, but she'd been at a loss as to how to deal with his restless yearning to rodeo. The more she tried to make him stay, the more he'd stayed away. True, he'd tried to get her to go with him, but Rozlyn had refused to leave the ranch for even a few days. Actually, she'd been afraid it would only encourage him to travel if she gave in and spent a few of her days and nights on the rodeo circuit with him. But now, looking back on it, she wondered what would have happened if she had. Would their love still be alive? Would they still be together?

The questions filled her with anguish as she and Jack jostled over the rough track leading back to the ranch house. It had been a long day and Jack had remained quiet for most of the afternoon. Now he drove in silence, one hand on the wheel, the other arm resting across the back of the seat. He'd pushed the brim of his black hat back off his forehead and his blond hair tumbled rakishly forward. In the falling twilight he looked incredibly young. As if no time had passed since the first day she met him.

She swallowed, then spoke. "Jack, if your being here is going to jeopardize your chances at another championship, then you shouldn't be here."

Jack turned to stare at her, trying to figure out what had prompted the unexpected remark. "Why do you say that?"

She shrugged in an effort to appear casual. "I—just wouldn't want to be responsible for—for knocking you out of all that money."

"I wouldn't think it even mattered to you."

"It doesn't," she hastily assured him. "I'm just trying to tell you that I don't hold you to anything. I mean, you're not responsible for my financial security just because a piece of paper says we're still married."

For a moment there, he'd thought perhaps that Rozlyn might be softening. That she might really care about what he did for a living and the coveted position he'd achieved in the PRCA. But obviously it wasn't that at all. She just didn't want to be beholden or tied to him in any way. The idea left him feeling very dejected.

"I used to mail checks to you regularly. Why did you never cash them?"

She looked away from him, out the window. The clouds had cleared and the evening star twinkled in the big Texas sky. As a child she used to make a wish on it. But she'd stopped believing in wishes a long time ago. "I didn't want your money, Jack. It was you I wanted."

The quiver of pain in her voice was unmistakable and took Jack by complete surprise. Had his leaving really hurt her that much? All this time he'd never thought of her wanting him or needing him. To think that she had shook him clear through. He'd never intended or wanted to hurt her. But he'd felt her ultimatum had left him no other choice.

In the first few months he'd sent her as much money as he could. Not as a way to replace the void his leaving had caused, but rather to help her with the ranch. That was what she had loved, not him. "You wanted me on your terms, Roz. Your conditions. I think you still do. I think if I tried to love you again, you'd still be the same way."

There was no anger in his voice. Rather, it was weary, desolate. The sound made Rozlyn unconsciously hug her arms around her waist.

With her face still turned to the window, she said,

"I guess it's a good thing we didn't make love this afternoon. You might have worried I'd try using it to hold you here. And you wouldn't like that, would you?"

Jack didn't know what he'd like anymore. When he'd run into Michael the other night in San Antonio, he'd been going freely from one town and one rodeo to the next, but he hadn't been happy. Slowly he was coming to the realization that his profession wasn't enough.

But damn it all, he'd tried once with Rozlyn and failed. If he'd come back to the Broken Spur unconsciously thinking Rozlyn was the thing he needed to make his life whole, something had gone haywire with his thinking. She'd made him crazy once. If he tried again with her and failed, he didn't think he could bear it.

"I don't know," he said, annoyed because he was so confused, and she was the cause of it. "Maybe we should make love and find out."

Just to hear him suggest such a thing had Rozlyn gripping the edge of the seat. "Not on your life, Jack! I can still see the wanderlust in your eyes. I don't mean to let you tear my life apart a second time."

Without looking her way, Jack tugged his hat brim back down on his forehead. Maybe she was right, but that didn't keep him from wanting to jam on the brakes and prove to her—and him—that at least physically she still loved him.

Rozlyn sighed with relief as the lights from the

ranch house appeared in the far distance. These emotional rides with Jack were draining her. Besides that, she was deeply afraid that if he decided they should become lovers again, she wouldn't be able to resist.

Later that night the telephone rang just as Rozlyn was getting out of the bathtub. Hurriedly throwing on her plaid bathrobe, she rushed to the kitchen to pick it up.

"Roz, is that you?"

The connection was full of crackly static. Rozlyn strained to hear the voice on the other end. "Michael?"

"Yeah, it's me. I just thought I'd call and see how things are going."

"Where are you?" she asked, shivering as she tried to wrap the robe closer around her damp body.

"I'm in Tulsa."

"At a rodeo?"

"It starts tomorrow night. At the civic center."

The line suddenly cleared and Rozlyn could hear the excitement lacing Michael's voice. It was the same sound Jack had always had when he talked about drawing a bull to ride that no one had ever ridden before.

"Is Pa okay?"

"He's fine."

"What about you, Sis? Did you get Sammy to come help you?"

Sammy was a college boy who had grown up with

Michael. He'd offered to help her around the ranch on his off days. Rozlyn hadn't bothered to call him.

"No. I can't afford him."

Her words must have knocked the wind from Michael, because there was a long pause. "Guess you're still blaming me for not being there to help you."

"No. I don't blame you. Don't worry about it."

After another long pause, Michael said, "I'm doing pretty good, Roz. I'm holding my money together. Maybe soon, I'll be able to send you some to help out with things."

Tears suddenly stung her throat. She loved her brother, and more than anything she wanted him to be happy. If he wanted a life apart from her, she would have to accept it. "I'm doing all right, Michael."

"Gee, Sis, I expected you to still be hollering for me to come home."

She almost smiled at the bewilderment in his voice. "I think we both realize my hollering wasn't going to change your mind."

"Uh—you'll never guess who I ran into down in San Antonio."

Rozlyn suddenly tensed. "Oh, yes. I know."

"You know I ran into Jack?" he asked in surprise.

Rozlyn hadn't planned on mentioning anything about Jack, but now that her brother had brought it up, she could hardly avoid it.

"Yes. He—he's here at the ranch."

There was a pregnant pause. When Michael spoke

again she could tell he was smiling from ear to ear.
"Jack's back home?"

Why did everyone say it that way? First her grandfather, then Margaret, now Michael. Annoyed, she
said, "I wouldn't put it that way, Michael. But he is
here—for the time being."

"But—doesn't that mean you're going to get back
together?"

"No. It doesn't. Look, Michael—"

"Sis, I think you love the guy!"

Footsteps sounded behind her. Rozlyn turned just in
time to see Jack entering the kitchen. She blushed as
his eyes slid over her with a familiarity that told her
he hadn't forgotten what she looked like underneath
her robe.

"I—don't want to go into this now," she said
tightly. "I'd rather hear about you."

He made a frustrated sound. "Put Jack on the
phone, will you? I'd like to talk to him."

"Michael," she began warningly. "I don't
think—"

"Oh, hell, Sis, I won't tell him you're still crazy
about him! He's probably going to find that out for
himself."

Angry now, Rozlyn didn't bother with a reply. She
stuck the phone out at Jack, who was busy pouring
himself a glass of orange juice.

"Jack, Michael wants to speak with you."

Surprised, Jack took the phone from her. "Hi, boy.
What's going on?"

As soon as Jack began to speak, Rozlyn left the room. She didn't want to be near him while he talked to her brother. Especially if Michael decided to tell him some insane thing like she still loved him.

Sometime later, a knock sounded on Rozlyn's bedroom door. Since she'd already gone to bed, she raised herself up on one elbow and switched on the bedside lamp.

"What is it?" she called.

For an answer Jack opened the door and stepped inside. Rozlyn unconsciously hugged the cover to her chin.

As Jack moved forward, he was as much aware of the room as he was of Rozlyn. Its familiar walls and furnishings swamped him with hot, sweet memories.

"What are you doing in here?"

"I want to talk to you."

"Can't it wait until morning, Jack?"

He stepped up beside the bed and folded his arms across his chest. Rozlyn noticed he'd changed his work shirt to a navy blue T-shirt. The thin material couldn't disguise the bulging muscles of his chest and arms. Rozlyn's eyes slid over them before lifting to his face.

Jack's mind barely registered her question. Seeing her in bed, the same bed they'd shared, was choking him with remembered pleasures.

"I don't want it to wait until morning," he said, his voice softly challenging. "I want to know why you didn't tell me you were in financial trouble?"

Rozlyn bolted upright, and the forgotten covers slid down to expose her lacy nightgown. "I'm not in financial trouble! Who told you that? If Pa—"

"Michael told me," he said grimly. Unable to stop them, his eyes wandered downward to the shape of her breasts beneath the blue lace.

She expelled a breath sharply. "He had no business telling you something like that!"

"He didn't volunteer the information. I asked him."

Rozlyn narrowed her eyes skeptically. "Why?"

"Because I had a suspicion something was wrong the minute you told me you'd sold Mighty Warrior."

Rozlyn's gaze fell away from his to fasten guiltily on the floor.

"I wish you'd forget about that damn horse," she muttered.

"I can't. I know how much you loved him. You wouldn't have gotten rid of him unless you had to."

"Look, Jack, I will admit the cash flow around here has been low. But I'm not in any dire situation. I've weathered worse storms than this." Which was true. Jack's leaving had been much worse for her than the lack of money she'd had lately.

"Damn it, Rozlyn, there's no need for you to scrape and scrimp. To get rid of your horse! All you had to do was tell me you needed help. Hell, I tried to give you money."

Her green eyes gleamed with a mixture of anger and tears. "You haven't been around to tell, Jack. Not that I would have anyway!"

Lifting his face toward the ceiling, Jack raked his fingers through his hair. "No, you probably wouldn't have," he said sardonically. "You have too much stubborn pride for that."

"My finances are none of your business," she bit back.

When Jack had left the ranch two years ago, Rozlyn had been solvent. He also knew she was anything but extravagant in her spending. When they'd been together, he'd virtually had to force her to buy things for herself.

Sinking onto the edge of the mattress, his eyes searched hers for answers. "What happened, Rozlyn?"

Rozlyn could not ignore the concern in his quietly spoken question. Still she didn't want to acknowledge it, either. He'd never cared about her. Not really, she thought bitterly. "This and that," she said evasively.

His gray eyes bored into hers, demanding a true answer. Shaken by the power of his gaze, Rozlyn had to look away from him. "Pa got pretty sick last year and insurance just isn't enough nowadays. Then—then we had a drought last summer in this part of the state. The grass dried up and all the ranchers around here had to start feeding two months ahead of schedule. And then a hard winter made me lose some cow-and-calf pairs. But the weather put a drain on everyone, not just me, Jack."

He understood that, but it didn't change anything. "Rozlyn, I've never been able to understand you. Why do you struggle so to hang on to this place? It's just a piece of ground. You're working yourself to death, and for what? Does this place give you that much happiness?''

She stared at him as though his questions were insulting. ''The Broken Spur is my home, Jack. Of course it makes me happy.''

His nostrils flared as he reached for her hand. ''You don't look like a happy person to me, Roz.''

He was so near to her that his knee was nearly touching her thigh. She felt threatened by his closeness, because she knew he was aware of just how much it affected her. In an attempt to put a bit of distance between them, she tried to pull her hand away, but he refused to release it.

The touch caused a tingling heat to rush up and down her arm, and beneath her breast her heart began a heavy thud, thud. ''Well, I am,'' she countered as evenly as she could. ''Just because a person doesn't go around laughing and smiling all the time doesn't mean he's unhappy.''

''I'll bet you haven't been off this place in days. I'll bet you haven't been out to eat or to see a movie in months.''

She made a deprecating sound. ''Movies these days aren't worth wasting your money on.''

His face wrinkled into a rueful frown. ''Especially if you don't have the money to spend in the first place. You know, Roz, I look at you and I see the same tired despair I saw on my mother's face when she and my father were struggling to hold on to their ranch down at Rosenberg. She worked like a dog, sacrificed all the things a woman shouldn't do without, just to hang on to a piece of ground and a herd of cows.''

Unknowingly, Rozlyn tightened her fingers around his as she took in his words. She understood that Jack had grown up feeling unloved and cast aside. And she knew that he blamed most of what happened to his family on the ranch they'd lost. But didn't he realize that it had been his folks, not the place, that had failed?

''Maybe I do put too much of myself into this place, Jack. But after our parents died, the Broken Spur was all Michael and I had. When—they drowned in that accident it was so sudden, so shocking. One day we were all a happy family, and the next—''

She broke off with a helpless shake of her head. ''In the days afterward, I came to realize that people don't last. Nothing lasts but the land. And I knew if I worked hard enough at it, it would always be there for me.''

Jack's eyes slipped over her features. They were softened by the dim glow of the bedside lamp. He found he wanted to lean forward and press his lips against the tender curve of her cheek. He wanted to whisper her name, to push her back against the pillows, to press his body into hers, to show that there were other things in life besides hard work, cows and land.

''If you'd worked as hard at keeping me, then maybe things would have been different for us, Rozlyn.'' He rubbed his thumb softly against the back of her hand. She couldn't know, he thought, just how much he wished things were different for the two of them. How he wished she could have loved him as much as the Broken Spur.

Rozlyn's green eyes filled with bewilderment then tears. She looked away from their entwined fingers and sucked in a painful breath. "Please leave me alone, Jack. I'm tired."

Jack started to say something else, then deciding against it, he rose from the bed. "I'll see you in the morning."

Rozlyn nodded, careful not to look at him.

As Jack went out the door, it struck him that he didn't want to leave her. God help him, he didn't know what was making him feel this way! He didn't know why he wanted to touch her, to make love to her, to make her smile and hear her laugh again. He'd believed all the feelings he'd ever had for Rozlyn had died. But apparently they hadn't. They were still alive inside of him. What in hell was he going to do about it?

Rozlyn watched the door close behind him, then fell weakly back against the pillows. Oh, God, what was happening to her? she wondered. For a minute there she'd wanted to tug Jack down on the bed beside her. She'd wanted to make love to him and know that in the morning his face would be on the pillow next to her.

Why did she want him still, after all he'd done to her? How could her body be so forgiving? Or was it her heart?

Chapter Five

Rozlyn slept badly again, but this time she'd set the alarm so as not to be late. From the window of her bedroom she could see the sun dawning on a clear sky. She was grateful for the break in the weather. It was not only better for the cattle but also better for her dull spirits. Maybe a little sunshine would put her in a better mood for Margaret's birthday party tonight.

After she'd dressed in a pair of black jeans and a red plaid shirt, she crossed the hall to the bathroom. On the way, she could see the door to Jack's room was open. His bed was empty, the covers already smoothed back into their proper place.

He was probably in the kitchen with Axton, she decided. For as long as Rozlyn could remember, her grandfather had risen every day at five o'clock to make coffee and listen to the livestock report on a local radio station. He was enjoying Jack's company, she knew. In the past two days he'd talked and showed more interest than he had in years. But it worried her to think how her grandfather was going to react once Jack left the ranch again.

"Good morning, Pa. Ready for breakfast?" she asked as she entered the warm kitchen.

"If I can have grits. Think you can cook me some?"

Rozlyn began to tie an apron over her jeans. "Yes. But not with gravy. And don't try to talk Jack into it, either," she warned the old man.

"He's gone down to the barn."

"Oh."

"Said he's gonna give that sorrel horse of yours a lesson in manners."

Rozlyn paused in the act of opening the refrigerator. "Jack doesn't need to bother with that horse."

Axton poured a bit of his coffee into a saucer. After it cooled a moment he carefully drank it. "Jack don't want him hurtin' you again."

Rozlyn grimaced as she bent to pull eggs and milk from the shelf. "I guess Jack told you about my fall yesterday."

"Yeah. He was worried about you, Sis."

Rozlyn's laugh was short and brittle. "Jack only worries about himself."

"That ain't so. You're just so bitter you can't see past the nose on your face. If the man only cared about himself, what's he doing here on the Broken Spur?''

Rozlyn wanted to know the answer to that herself.

By the time Rozlyn had breakfast ready, Jack still hadn't returned to the house. Rather than waiting on him and serving the meal cold, she donned a heavy coat and went down to the barn to find him.

The sun was just bursting over a stand of mesquite trees on the eastern horizon. Pink-orange fingers of light spread across the barnyard and connecting corrals. In one of the lots, Jack was reining the sorrel in a tight circle. He handled the horse with an ease that came from natural instinct and long hours in the saddle.

He spotted her as she approached the fence. As her long legs carried her gracefully forward, her chestnut hair swung freely about her shoulders.

Rozlyn had dominated his thoughts for the bigger part of the night. The way she'd looked last night in bed, the things she'd said, and the hurt she'd tried to hide when she talked about her parents. He'd never realized just how much their deaths had affected her until last night. He was beginning to understand, or least partly so, why she was so determined to cling to the ranch. Why in her own demanding way, she'd tried to hold on to him.

Rozlyn climbed up on the fence and Jack pulled the horse to a stop just a few inches away from her.

''Mornin', ma'am,'' he said with a grin, and a finger touched to the brim of his hat.

She had to smile back at him. His gallant greeting

demanded it. "Good morning. I see you've been taking Buster for a few rounds."

Jack reached out and gave the horse's neck a couple of affectionate pats. "I think we're beginning to understand each other."

The morning was still and cold. Jack's face was reddened by it, and his breath created clouds of vapor in the air around his face. His lips were whitened by the cold, but as Rozlyn's eyes dwelled on them she could only think of the heat they could bring to her, the mindless pleasure she felt each time he kissed her.

Determined to put the erotic thought out of her mind, she said, "I came to tell you that breakfast was ready."

"Oh. I didn't realize I'd been down here that long." Swinging his right leg over the saddle horn, he slid lithely to the ground. "I guess Axton's getting impatient to eat."

"I told him to go ahead without us," she said.

"Just let me get Buster out of the cold," Jack told her, "and I'll be finished here."

Rozlyn waited while Jack returned the horse to its stall. Once he'd finished the task and latched the barn door behind him, the two of them began to walk back to the house.

"How's your shoulder this morning?"

"It's fine," Rozlyn answered. "Just a little stiff. Thank you for asking."

"I pulled a ligament in my shoulder last year out

at Reno," he said. "It was hell for a while. I had to quit riding for a month."

Rozlyn had never dwelled on the danger involved in Jack's sport. She'd always tried not to. Bull riders were killed. Not frequently. But they did sometimes lose their lives to an angry horn, a misguided hoof, or simply by being slammed against the ground or the bucking chutes with the force of a two-thousand-pound animal.

She couldn't bear to think of Jack being injured, not even in a minor way. "What did you do while you were waiting to heal? Went a little crazy, I'll bet."

He laughed. "A little," he confessed. "I didn't know what to do with myself. When you get used to climbing on two or three bulls a week, anything less is pretty dull. But I survived. I've got an apartment in Houston so I went back to it to recuperate. Driving the freeways down there is almost like riding a bull anyway," he joked.

Anything less is pretty dull. That one phrase hung in her mind. It told Rozlyn more than he realized. Jack Barnett would find life with her here on the Broken Spur boring.

Well, Rozlyn, she told herself, you knew that all along. Just because he said he wanted to make love to you doesn't mean he's a changed man.

So why did some of the joy suddenly go out of seeing the morning sun?

Rozlyn fastened the skirt at the back of her waist, then stood back to inspect her image in the mirror.

The skirt and matching blouse were fashioned from an Aztec print of rust and turquoise on a beige background. It wasn't new by any means, but it was one of the few dresses she owned. She'd purchased it last summer for a church social. Since then she'd probably worn it twice.

The knowledge had her mind going back to the things Jack had said last night. He'd made it sound like a crime because she didn't involve her life in other things outside of the ranch. But what more did she want? she asked herself as she reached for a silver-colored concha belt.

She wasn't into socializing or partying. And even if she was, she didn't have the time or money for it. So what else did she need in her life?

She needed someone to love her, a little voice inside her answered. She needed someone to share things, to have a baby with, to make a real, stable family. Those things were all she'd ever wanted.

Jack was in the den, helping Axton on with his coat when Rozlyn appeared in the doorway.

"Are you both ready to go?" she asked the two men.

Jack looked around at the sound of her voice and immediately his breath caught in his throat. She looked beautiful, soft, feminine. Her long legs were covered with silky stockings and her feet were encased in a pair of dainty beige pumps. The sides of her hair were swept up and back and secured with a pair of combs.

As he and Axton drew near to her, Jack could see she was wearing the copper earrings and cuff bracelet he'd once given her as a gift. The pair matched the combs in her hair. He was stunned to see that she'd kept the jewelry, much less worn it tonight.

"I'm ready as I'll ever be," Axton grumbled. "If you ask me, this is a lot of fuss just because one old woman is turning seventy-five."

"Pa, you're a terrible old man," Rozlyn scolded. "I don't see what Margaret sees in you."

"Humph," he snorted. "She knows a good man when she sees one. Now where's my Stetson? You ain't been lettin' the rats chew on it, have you?"

Jack looked over at Rozlyn, who was standing on the other side of her grandfather. Her expression told him she wasn't sure if she wanted to laugh or curse. Then she turned her eyes to meet Jack's and smiled back at him. The smile was a shared intimacy, the closest thing to a kiss she could have given him. The sight of it made him feel warm, almost wanted.

"No, Pa. Your hat is hanging where it's been for the past ten years, on the rack by the front door. We'll get it on our way out," she patiently assured him.

On the way into town Axton exclaimed over Jack's luxurious truck. While the two men discussed the advantages of the vehicle, Rozlyn stared out at the night and tried not to notice Jack's thigh just a fraction away from hers.

He was looking extremely handsome tonight in a pair of black jeans and a Navajo printed shirt. Its flamboyant deep purple, red and black suited him. Jack had always projected the image of a man who lived on the edge, one who dared to do his own thing.

Rozlyn suddenly wondered what everyone was going to think when they saw him. Would they naturally assume that the two of them were back together? When Jack had left two years ago, she hadn't really discussed their problems with anyone other than Margaret. It was anyone's guess as to how they would greet Jack.

Margaret's party was being given by her daughter Peggy, a woman as large and lively as her mother. Rozlyn had always been fond of Peggy and her husband, Leo. The couple lived in a large split-level home on the outskirts of town. The minute Peggy met them at the door, she grabbed Jack and kissed him on the cheek.

"Jack Barnett, you are a sight for sore eyes! Wait till Leo sees you!"

As Peggy ushered them into the house, Rozlyn glanced over at Jack. He seemed to be just as bemused at Peggy's warm greeting as Rozlyn was. For her part, she was wondering at the way Margaret and Peggy were welcoming him home like some unsung hero. Didn't they remember the man had walked out on her? It made her wonder how they had really viewed Rozlyn's side of things.

Food was laid out on tables in nearly every room, including a large game room where many couples were dancing to recorded music. Axton quickly took himself off to a table where several of his old cronies were playing poker. Rozlyn was relieved that her grandfather would be pacified for a while, but she wasn't relishing the idea of being left to make the rounds with Jack.

"You two go ahead and find yourselves whatever you'd like to eat," Peggy told them. "Leo smoked a brisket so if it isn't all eaten, his feelings will be hurt."

Rozlyn smiled. "I'll be sure to eat some."

"Peggy," someone in the crowd called, "we need more ice over here."

The redheaded woman glanced apologetically at Rozlyn and Jack. "Sorry, I hear my name being called. I'll catch up with you later."

As the woman moved away from them, Jack curved his arm around Rozlyn's waist. "Come on, let's go find something to eat," he told her. "I'm starving."

On their way to one of the buffet tables, several people called out to them. Jack smiled and greeted them all as easily as if he'd never been away from Llano. Rozlyn wondered if they were all presuming she and Jack were back together. She supposed it would be a natural assumption to make. Especially with him holding on to her as if she belonged to him!

They were filling their plates with barbecue and other rich food when a familiar voice sounded beside Rozlyn.

"Roz, honey, I'm so glad you came tonight!"

Rozlyn looked up from her half-filled plate to see her longtime friend. "Connie, I didn't know you were going to be here! When did you get into town?"

"Just last night. I'm staying with Mom while Richard moves the last of our things from Austin."

"Oh, you're moving back to Llano?"

Connie nodded and smiled. "We didn't much like city life and now that we have the baby, we wanted to be closer to our parents so they could enjoy him."

Rozlyn glanced to her right to see that Jack had moved on toward the end of the table. Connie followed her gaze.

"When did Jack come back? Mom didn't mention anything to me about it."

Rozlyn continued to fill her plate. "He's only been here a few days. Your mother probably didn't know."

"Is he—going to stay?" Connie asked in a low voice.

Rozlyn had gone to school with Connie throughout grade school and high school. As friends they'd shared many good times. Each of them had married at the same age. Connie's marriage had worked out grandly. Rozlyn's hadn't.

"Uh—for a while," Rozlyn answered evasively. She didn't want to get into a conversation about her marriage tonight. Especially with Jack only a few feet away.

"He looks gorgeous, Roz," Connie whispered,

close to Rozlyn's face. "I think I'd swoon dead if Richard looked like that."

"Connie!" Rozlyn scolded under her breath. "Your husband is a wonderful man. He loves you utterly."

Connie grinned. "I know, but Jack is so—so movie starrish."

That was true enough, Rozlyn thought bitterly, because he was definitely not husband material. "Well, why don't you go tell him that?" she said a little tersely.

Connie laughed at her friend. "I think I'll just do that."

Rozlyn watched her friend move down the table to where Jack was filling a cup with coffee. She couldn't hear what her friend was saying, but from the laughter on Jack's face he must have found it amusing.

"Bet you were surprised to see Connie here, weren't you?"

Rozlyn looked around to see Margaret standing by her elbow. "Margaret, happy birthday! Are you having a good time?"

"Thank you, dear, I'm having a wonderful time. I wonder why you look like you aren't?"

Rozlyn drew in a long breath and moved on down the long table of food. Margaret followed her. "I just got here, Margaret. Give me time."

"Axton's already won a round of poker." Margaret laughed fondly. "The old geezer insisted he didn't want to come tonight, but I know better."

"Everyone seems so happy to see Jack again," Rozlyn couldn't help but say.

Margaret's brows lifted questioningly. "And why shouldn't they? Jack always was a likable man. There isn't anyone in this room he wouldn't help if they needed it. People around here don't forget that."

The older woman's eyes narrowed. "Why? Would it make you feel better if they gave him the cold shoulder? My God, Rozlyn, surely you don't have that much bitterness in you."

Grimacing, Rozlyn shook her head. "I'm just wondering why they remember what a likable man he is, but they can't seem to remember that the man walked out on his wife."

Margaret clicked her tongue. "Roz, everyone here knows there's two sides to every story. They've given Jack the benefit of the doubt, just as they have you."

Rozlyn stared at the older woman. She'd never imagined that people outside her family had viewed the breakup of their marriage as a two-sided thing. She'd never viewed it that way. She'd always believed Jack had left the ranch because he'd wanted to. But maybe everyone else believed she'd pushed Jack off the ranch. It was an idea that stunned her.

Rozlyn opened her mouth to question Margaret, but her son-in-law, Leo, was suddenly grabbing the older woman's elbow.

"Excuse us, will you, Roz. The birthday girl is wanted in the kitchen."

She nodded at Leo, then turned to finish filling her

plate. Once she was finished she joined Connie, who was sitting with Jack at a table on the other side of the room.

"I'll let you have your husband back," Connie said with a wide smile as Rozlyn approached the two. "I've got to go check on Jonathan."

"You brought the baby with you?" Rozlyn asked eagerly.

Connie vacated her folding chair and motioned for Rozlyn to take it. "Yes, he's in one of the back bedrooms and I'm afraid I won't be able to hear him if he wakes and cries."

"I'll come to see him later," she promised Connie as the other woman moved away.

Jack positioned his chair closer to Rozlyn, then took a bite of brisket. Even though he wasn't touching her, she could feel his closeness, smell his spicy cologne.

"Connie tells me that she and Richard have been living in Austin for the past year," he said.

"That's right. He was working as a city policeman there, but they decided to come back. I'm glad. I've missed her."

It was much more than she'd ever said to *him,* Jack thought. But then maybe she hadn't missed his company. Maybe after he left the Broken Spur, she'd put him totally from her mind.

Admittedly, these past two years he'd convinced himself that he didn't miss Rozlyn or anything about their marriage. But now he knew he'd been lying to himself. All the little things about her, living with her, were coming back to him. And he was beginning to realize how much those little things could mean.

A few minutes later, he was talking to an old friend when he saw Rozlyn leave the game room.

"I'll talk to you later about that cow, Will," he told the tall man standing next to him, then quickly exited the crowded room.

As he neared the back of the house, he could hear Rozlyn's voice coming from a bedroom on the left. The door was ajar and he reached to push it open, but he paused as he heard what she was saying.

"He's so beautiful, Connie. I can't imagine having such a precious child."

"You know, Roz, I always wondered why you and Jack didn't have a baby. Didn't he want one?"

The little sound that passed Rozlyn's lips was a broken one. "I wanted one desperately, but—Jack. Well, I could see he didn't want to be a family man. He was having trouble being a husband and I was afraid if I even mentioned the idea of making him a father he would turn tail and run." Her short laugh was a hard one. "Isn't that ironic? He turned tail and ran anyway."

"Oh Roz, I'm—not so sure—"

The baby began to cry, cutting off Connie's reply. Jack stood immobilized. He'd never known Rozlyn had wanted a baby. She'd never talked to him about having a child, and he'd presumed she didn't want one. In fact, he'd believed she didn't love him enough to want his child. But now, oh, God, he'd just heard her say something entirely different.

Whimpers were still coming from inside the room. Jack used the interrupted moment to enter the room.

Both women were sitting on the edge of the bed. Between them on a small square blanket was Connie's infant son.

"What's the matter with him? Is he sick?" Jack asked.

Connie laughed. "He's mad because I changed his diaper."

Jack bent over the baby. "Hey, there, boy, are you going to be a lawman like your daddy?"

The moment Jack began talking, the baby hushed his fussing and stared wide-eyed up at him.

Connie groaned. "Richard already calls him his little deputy. But I told him Jonathan's going to be a scientist or an architect."

Little Jonathan began to wave his arms happily in the air. When Jack touched the baby's hand, he was amazed at how the tiny fingers gripped his large one.

"Why, with a grip like that he'll be riding bulls by the time he's fifteen," Jack assured the two women.

Rozlyn rolled her eyes, albeit good-naturedly, and Connie laughed.

"Oh, no. For the first twenty years of his life, my baby's not getting on anything more than a tricycle."

Peggy poked her head around the door. "Connie, can you come here for a minute? You've got to settle a squabble. There's a couple of guys out here that don't believe Richard is going to run for sheriff. They won't believe me when I tell them he is.''

Connie rose from the bed. "Can you watch Jonathan for a minute or two?" she asked Rozlyn.

"Sure, I'd be glad to."

After Connie disappeared, Jack sat down on the edge of the bed and looked over at Rozlyn. Her eyes were on the baby, and the wistful expression on her face was more than obvious to him.

"He's something, isn't he?" Jack spoke quietly. "I never realized they were this small at the beginning. What do you suppose he weighs?"

Rozlyn glanced over at Jack, then back to the baby. "Oh, I'd say maybe twelve or thirteen pounds."

"Lord, that's a tiny little critter. Do you figure I was ever that little?" he mused aloud.

Rozlyn laughed softly. "I figure you were even smaller than this at one time in your life, Jack. You weren't always a big, brawny bull rider."

Jonathan decided it was time to make more noise. When he began to cry in earnest, Rozlyn picked him up. "Would you hand me his bottle, Jack? I believe Connie put it back in the diaper bag."

He found the bag, then handed Rozlyn the bottle. She cuddled the baby to her breast and offered him the bottle. He latched onto it with an eagerness that made Jack laugh.

"Looks like he likes his groceries."

Rozlyn smoothed the fine, dark baby hair covering Jonathan's head. "He's a growing boy."

Seeing Rozlyn with the baby in her arms was a new experience for Jack. And he'd never realized until this moment, just how much he'd given up the day he'd walked away from her.

"You look right like that, Rozlyn. With a baby in your arms."

Rozlyn felt an ache of emotion fill her throat as she looked down at the child in her arms. It would have felt right to have had your child, Jack, she thought. "You think so?"

"I often thought about you and I having a child. But I guess you didn't know that."

His words were such a complete surprise that Rozlyn stared at him for a long second. "No, I didn't know that."

Jack's mouth twisted ruefully. "I know I didn't have much fathering, and I don't know much of what a father's supposed to do or be, but I would have loved our child, Roz. No matter what, I would have loved it."

Jack's admission pierced her heart. Her eyes stung with tears of regret. Maybe Jack had been right when he'd said she hadn't known him. Maybe he'd been right about more than that; Rozlyn just didn't know anymore.

"I didn't think you wanted to be a father," she murmured, then lifted her eyes to meet his gaze.

The wetness of her green eyes tore at everything inside him. "You didn't think I wanted to be a husband either. But I did."

She didn't want to hear that. Not now. Now that it was too late to change the past.

"Jack, don't—" Her words halted as Connie reentered the room.

"Well, here I am again," Connie said cheerfully. "How's my son? Giving you guys problems?"

Something far deeper than that, Rozlyn thought ruefully as she handed the baby back to his mother.

Aloud she said, "Not at all."

Jack got to his feet and Rozlyn glanced over at him. "We'd better get out of here so she can put him to sleep."

He nodded in agreement and the two of them left the room.

For the next hour Rozlyn mixed and mingled with the other guests, many of whom she hadn't seen in weeks. She listened to stories about everything from the high school basketball team to a local farmer who broke his leg while trying to get out of his muddy pigpen.

Any other time Rozlyn would have enjoyed the conversation and merrymaking, but tonight her heart just wasn't in it. She could think of nothing but Jack and the things he'd said to her. He'd exposed a part of himself that she'd never seen before, and it had left her shaken and totally confused.

She was talking to Peggy when Leo came up and whirled his wife away onto the dance floor.

As Rozlyn watched him pull her away, Jack spoke

in her ear. "Leo has a good idea. How about a dance?"

"I don't think so."

"Why?"

She gave him a sidelong glance. "Because I—I've forgotten how," she said quickly.

Jack's smile was wicked. "Now is the perfect time to find out."

"Jack! I said—"

He tugged on her arm and Rozlyn knew she couldn't say more without making a scene, so she allowed him to pull her toward the end of the room that had been cleared of furniture. Two more couples along with Peggy and Leo were dancing in the small space, but Rozlyn still felt very conspicuous as Jack pulled her into his arms.

Rozlyn had only danced a very few times in her life, and with Jack she'd always felt as if she had two left feet. He had an inborn rhythm and grace that made dancing come as naturally as breathing to him. Rozlyn knew those were the two qualities that had not only made him a good dancer but a good bull rider, as well. It was a sport that required a sense of rhythm and timing, a grace and balance that would catch a judge's eye.

The talent had taken him a long way, she thought. All the way to the top. And the top was a long way from Llano and the Broken Spur.

Jack could feel the taut stiffness of her body as he moved her around the floor. "You're not really that worried about stepping on my toes, are you?'' he teased.

"You know me, Jack. I never was much of a dancer."

Jack pulled her closer, so that her body was pressed to the length of his. Rozlyn felt utterly helpless as the hard warmth of him turned her bones to mush.

He laughed softly, his breath fanning her cheek. "It's not any harder than riding Buster, Roz."

She looked up and discovered his face not much more than an inch away. Even though they were barely moving, she felt as breathless as if she'd been running. Her eyes moved from his gray ones down to the firm line of his lips.

At the moment he was smiling at her and his white teeth glinted at the corner of his mouth. Her fingers unconsciously tightened on his. "You'll never let me live that down. You've probably told everyone here tonight that I got bucked off."

His expression innocent, he shook his head. "I haven't told anyone."

She didn't say anything to that, and for a few moments they were both silent as they continued to move to the slow music.

"Uh—I suppose everyone has been asking you what you're doing back in Llano," she said.

His eyes searched her face. "No. I think everyone knows the reason I'm back here. You."

Her eyes widened. "Me? You didn't come here for me."

No. Not for her exactly. But she was the reason that had pulled him back to West Texas. "I came back to help you," he reasoned.

"That's not what they're thinking and you know it," she said, deliberately looking away from him. She spied Margaret standing to one side of the room. The older woman was looking straight at her and Jack. The smug smile on her face spoke volumes.

"Does that bother you?"

Jack's gravelly voice pulled her eyes back around to him. Bother her, she thought. It made her think of things she shouldn't be thinking, wishing for things that would ultimately hurt her. "It makes me uncomfortable. All of them are probably thinking we're sleeping together."

Jack frowned. "Most husbands and wives do sleep together," he pointed out. "It's a normal occurrence."

"There's nothing normal about us," Rozlyn reminded him.

"And you blame all that on me, don't you?" Jack countered.

For the past two years she'd blamed him. Now she didn't know if her way of thinking had been entirely fair. "I—don't want us to argue, Jack. Not here. Not tonight."

"You're right," he said, suddenly smiling at her. "We're here at Margaret's party to have fun."

He pulled his fingers away from hers to touch the corners of her lips. "So come on," he coaxed, "smile for me."

Slowly Rozlyn's lips curved upward until eventually they parted on a gurgle of laughter. "How's that?" she asked him.

It was perfect, Jack thought. It was the way he'd always wanted her to be while they'd been living together. Happy, smiling, laughing. But after a while he'd had to face the fact that he wasn't the man who could make her happy, much less keep her happy.

It would be crazy of him to think he could now. But as he held her close in his arms, pressed his cheek against her silky hair, he couldn't help but wish he could be the man to put joy into her life.

Chapter Six

The next morning when Rozlyn entered the kitchen, she found Axton eating a bowl of cornflakes.

"It's about time you woke up. Is that what nightlife does to you, girly? Makes you sleep till noon?"

Rozlyn deliberately looked at the clock on the wall. The black arms told them both it was six-thirty. "Doesn't look like noon to me. But I'm surprised to see you up. I thought all that hard poker playing last night would have done you in."

She went to the cabinet for a coffee mug. Behind her at the table Axton gave her a toothless grin. "I won more than twelve dollars last night."

"Twelve dollars! I thought you were playing with pennies!"

Axton cackled with glee. "We were. But none of

them guys could ever figure out if I was bluffing or not.''

Rozlyn shook her head before taking a careful sip of the steaming coffee. ''Where's Jack?''

''I think he's back on that red horse this morning. He's been gone more than an hour now, I'd say.''

Sighing, she went over to the kitchen window and looked out. The morning was clear but cold. From this angle she could see part of the barn and the corral on the west end. Jack was nowhere in sight.

Damn it, she'd gone to sleep thinking about the man. Now she was starting the day the same way. It couldn't go on like this. She couldn't allow it!

A half hour later she was putting breakfast on the table when Jack came through the back door. From the corner of her eye she watched him hang his hat and duster on the rack by the door. He was dressed warmly this morning in a heavy brown sweater with bright Santa Fe designs striping the chest.

He looked over at Rozlyn and smiled. ''Good morning.''

The sight of him lifted her heart. It was something she could no longer deny. ''Good morning,'' she greeted. ''Breakfast is ready if you are.''

''As soon as I wash,'' he assured her.

Rozlyn waited for him to return from the bathroom before she poured the coffee. It was the first thing he reached for after taking his seat opposite her.

''Where's Axton? Isn't he going to eat?'' Jack asked.

"I didn't get up until six-thirty, so Pa got tired of waiting and ate a bowl of cornflakes."

Jack chuckled. "That old man hasn't changed a bit. He's still as crotchety as ever."

Rozlyn's smile was full of fondness. "Yes, he is. But I'd miss him terribly if he wasn't around."

Jack looked at her bent head. He knew how much Rozlyn adored her grandfather.

"Axton will probably live to be a hundred," he assured her. "He's too ornery not to."

Rozlyn had cooked biscuits and milk gravy this morning. Along with that she'd set out the butter and honey, because she remembered how well Jack had always liked it.

She assured herself the thoughtful act wasn't a sign she was giving in and forgiving him. She'd just decided that it wouldn't hurt anything to be civil to the man if he was going to feed the cattle and break her horse for her.

As Jack spread a biscuit with butter, he said, "I'm going into town after I finish with breakfast. Would you like to go?"

Surprise brought her eyes up to his. "To town?"

He nodded. "I thought you might need some things."

Rozlyn shook her head. What little she needed could be put off. "I just stocked the kitchen with groceries a few days ago. Why are you going to town?"

"Oh, to get a few things," he told her.

She watched him drizzle honey over the hot bread. "What kind of things?"

"Just this and that. It won't take me long, I'll be back in plenty of time to help you with the feeding."

Rozlyn wasn't worried about that. She'd merely been curious about his wants. Thank goodness he hadn't realized that, she thought. "Pa said you were back on Buster this morning," she remarked.

"I was. I rode some of the fencing. That north fence by the pond needs some repair work."

"I know. I—just haven't had a chance to get to it," she said, which was true enough. She wasn't going to tell him she was too low on funds to buy barbed wire and fence posts. "Besides, I don't necessarily need that pasture right now."

"Not now. But you will when the grass starts coming."

Spring, she thought wistfully. It was always a time she looked forward to. The leaves and grass and wildflowers made the ranch look beautiful again. As the days grew hotter and hotter, the huge cottonwood at the corner of the house would once again shade the kitchen. The cows would stand in the pond, and Axton would move his card table to the front porch. And as for herself, she'd get a breather from work until haying season began.

Jack would surely be gone by then. If she could see into the future, she'd more than likely see that he'd be gone in another week or two.

Would she be glad to see him go? The question

brought a hollow ache to her heart, and as she looked across the table at him, she knew that she was in trouble. That somewhere along the way she'd started seeing him in a different light.

She'd begun to think of him as her husband again. And that was a dangerous thing to do. Jack didn't want to be a husband. He hadn't come back vowing to love her, to stay on the ranch and build the home and family she'd always wanted. No, she had to be realistic about things. She had to remember that Jack was a rodeo rider, not a family man.

While Jack was gone to town, Rozlyn decided to use the time to clean house. She rarely had the chance to do indoor chores, and the neglect showed in every room of the house.

After the breakfast dishes were washed and put away, she began to strip the sheets from all the beds. Jack had already straightened the covers on his bed. She pulled them off anyway and tossed the bundle of white sheets into a laundry basket she'd carried with her.

Looking around the room, she noticed that Jack hadn't changed his neat habits. He'd never been one to throw dirty clothes on the floor or scatter personal items around where they didn't belong. A habit he'd once told her that had been instilled by the strict and formidable aunt who'd raised him.

A gray Stetson was placed neatly on its crown on top of the chest of drawers. Next to it was a wide leather belt. Rozlyn drew nearer the chest as she spotted the buckle attached to the end of it.

Something, she wasn't sure what, compelled her to pick it up for a closer inspection. It was a trophy buckle. Jack's name and the year were printed on it, along with the words PRCA Champion Bull Rider. The oval buckle was made of gold and silver, but even Rozlyn knew that wasn't the reason it was so coveted. It took extraordinary talent to win it. Many tried for years and never came close. Jack had done it in a relatively short time.

She hadn't seen the buckle on him since he'd been back home and she wondered why. She'd been so against his rodeoing that it surprised her that he didn't want to flaunt his success in her face.

With saddened eyes she traced the edge of the buckle with her forefinger. She'd fought Jack hard about his riding, and at the time she'd believed it was the right thing to do. She'd given him the final ultimatum of leaving the sport or leaving her. Had she been unfair? Had it been asking too much of him?

Michael had often told her so. But then Michael had always been in alliance with Jack. Now that she thought about it, everyone but her seemed to be in alliance with Jack.

"I didn't know you wanted the sheets washed or I would've taken them off this morning."

Jumping at the unexpected sound of Jack's voice, she turned to face him. "I—was just looking at your buckle. It's very beautiful."

Jack saw that she was still cradling it in her two palms, almost in a reverent way. He was as puzzled as he was surprised by her demeanor. "I'm surprised you'd say that."

Her eyes left his face and dropped back to the intricate engraving on the precious metal. "Why didn't you wear it last night? Aren't you proud of it?"

One corner of his mouth lifted. "Of course I am. But I'm not a showy person. I think you know that."

No, he might have a large dose of male arrogance, but he'd never been a braggart. She placed the belt and buckle back on the chest. When she turned around, she discovered Jack had moved to within inches of her. As always, every nerve in her body began to quiver in wild reaction to his nearness.

"I can't understand you, Roz," he said softly. "Sometimes it's almost like a part of you is proud of my achievements."

"A part of me *is* proud, Jack." Her throat was so tight it hurt to say the words. She looked into his eyes and saw that she'd bewildered him even more.

"Roz, I—"

She quickly shook her head. "I'm not saying anything new, Jack. I've always been proud of you."

His gray eyes softened, and he reached out to touch her face as though he were seeing her for the first time. "You hate what I do. You've told me so time again."

The pain in his voice was impossible to ignore, yet Rozlyn wished she couldn't hear it. She didn't want to think that Jack hurt. Or that maybe she'd been the cause of his pain.

These past two years he'd been away, Rozlyn had only thought of *her* pain, her loss. It was a shock to think that Jack might have been suffering, too.

"I hated it because it took you away from me," she said in a small voice.

Jack began shaking his head. "Why do you only see things in black and white? There's more than just two sides to life. More than just right or wrong!"

Anger surfaced in Rozlyn. Who was Jack to tell her about right or wrong? He was the one who'd walked and taken the easy way out!

Determined not to get into a shouting match, she brushed around him, then bent to pick up the laundry basket. "I don't want to talk about this, Jack. It's useless anyway."

She'd taken three steps when Jack's hand reached out and caught her upper arm. "It's useless because you're determined to be single-minded!"

Rozlyn's sharp laugh sliced him like a razor. "And you're not? Aren't you the man who refused to give me the home and husband I wanted?"

"What do you want, Rozlyn? A man who will kow-tow to every demand you make? Is that what you think love is?"

Her green eyes took on an icy edge. "I think it means being loyal and devoted. I never saw that from you."

The stiff anger on his face was replaced by utter

disbelief. "And you think I got loyalty and devotion from you?" He laughed harshly. "When are you going to grow up and realize that marriage is a two-way street?"

Rozlyn was so outraged she dropped the laundry basket and lashed out at him with both fists. "You're despicable! Hateful!"

One fist managed to strike his shoulder, the other he caught easily before it landed in the middle of his chest. "The truth hurts, doesn't it?" he asked tightly, his face looming down over hers.

"What truth? Yours?"

Jack's grip on her fist loosened as something else flared in his eyes. "I'm to blame for a lot of our problems," he whispered fiercely. "But, by God, I wasn't alone in it!"

Rozlyn tried to take in his words, but her knees were growing weak, her breaths coming in rapid jerks. She didn't know or care what he was saying anymore. All she could think about was the sight of his hard mouth only a fraction away from hers.

"Jack—"

His name came out more like a whimper. The yielding sound of it brought Jack's lips hungrily down on hers.

Rozlyn met the hard grinding of his mouth with a need that seconded his. Heat washed up and through her body, driving everything else from her mind. When he kissed her, held her, it made her forget all the pain and doubt she was feeling.

She arched her body against his as she lifted her hands to his neck. Jack wrapped his arms around her waist, drawing her into the tight circle of his embrace. His teeth grazed her upper lip, causing Rozlyn to involuntarily tighten her fingers on his neck.

Beneath the sweater she could feel the warmth and strength of his muscles. But the garment was a frustrating barrier when her hands itched to feel his skin. Urgently she moved them downward, then slipped them beneath the bottom of the material, where they encountered the hot, corded flesh at his waist.

Jack gasped against her lips. "Rozlyn, you don't know what you're doing!"

"Yes, I do Jack," she whispered breathlessly. "I know that I don't want to fight with you."

She slid her hands upward until the palms flattened against both his nipples. Jack shuddered and closed his eyes. He wished more than anything that he could shut the door, carry her to the bed and make hot, passionate love to her. But he knew that once their bodies were satiated they would be back to where they'd been a few minutes ago—throwing blame and accusations at each other.

He thrust her from him and drew in a ragged breath. Rozlyn looked blankly up at him, and the desire still clouding her eyes almost caused him to pull her back into his arms.

"You were right yesterday, Roz. Sex isn't going to change things between us."

But it wouldn't be sex, she thought desperately. It

would be making love. She reached out to him in an effort to convey what she was feeling, but Jack turned away and hurried out of the room.

The pain of Jack's rejection was deep and over-whelming. Minutes ticked away as she stared at the empty doorway, hoping her sheer will would conjure him back into the room. But after a while she realized he was not coming back. Not to the room and not to her.

Tears burned her eyes and she couldn't understand why. She didn't want Jack back in her life. He obviously didn't love her. He thought she was selfish and immature. He believed she was narrow-minded and unwilling to bend. She wasn't! Was she?

Wiping at her eyes, she crossed the room to where an oak bureau stood against the wall. On it was a photo Michael kept there of their parents. Their arms were around each other, their faces smiling at the camera.

Rozlyn's heart ached with regret as she picked up the gold frame and studied the two people who'd brought her into the world. She knew she needed them now more than she ever had in her life. She needed their guidance, their support. But they were lost to her forever. Perhaps Jack was, too.

The thought was a desolate one.

Jack kicked the last roll of barbed wire off the pickup bed, then jumped off the truck and shoved the tailgate back into place. He'd come back from town anxious to show Rozlyn the supplies he'd purchased for the ranch. Now he was wondering why he'd bought them in the first place. Rozlyn didn't appreciate his help. She didn't appreciate anything about him.

His frustrated thoughts were interrupted by the shrill whinny of a horse. He turned around to see Buster pacing the fence, his head and tail thrown high in the air. He had the heart of an outlaw, one that Jack doubted he could change.

The idea brought back the memory of Rozlyn falling headfirst into the arroyo. His fear at that moment had been so overwhelming it had sickened him. And then later back in the house when he'd questioned her about her shoulder, they'd come very close to making love. He'd wanted her so badly he'd ached with it.

Hell, he'd wanted her today in the bedroom. But he'd be damned before he let Rozlyn set terms and conditions on their relationship. She'd tried to do it in the past, and she was still trying to do it.

Still, it had taken something out of him to walk away from her. And even now his heart grew soft when he remembered the way she'd held his buckle, the way her voice had sounded when she'd said she was proud of him. He'd never expected that from her.

Sighing wearily, he took off his hat and ran his fingers through his hair. Rozlyn was such a contradiction—saying one thing with her body and another with her words. He didn't know what to think or believe anymore.

"Where did all this come from?"

Slapping his hat back onto his head, he looked around to see Rozlyn standing just outside the fence. She was dressed in jeans, boots and a red hooded sweatshirt. Her hair hung in a loose braid over one shoulder. She was as beautiful like this, he thought, as she had been last night in a dress, her young face enhanced with makeup.

"I bought it. At the hardware store," Jack said.

Rozlyn opened the gate and walked around the stack of lumber and sheets of corrugated iron. "I can't pay for this."

"It's already paid for. Don't worry about it."

Slowly she moved to the rolls of barbed wire and metal fence posts. It was like a gift from heaven. But how could she accept it from him?

"Jack, this isn't right."

"Why?"

She looked at him as if she couldn't believe he had to ask the question. "Because—it just isn't."

He propped one boot upon the back bumper. Resting his arm on his bent knee, he leveled his eyes on her face. "We're still married. Don't tell me what rights I have. If I want to invest in this place, I will."

She hadn't come down here looking for an argument. She was sick of arguing. "That's not what I meant," she said.

His brows lifted. "Then what did you mean?"

She moved closer to him. "I—don't want you to spend money on the ranch because you feel sorry for me."

To her surprise he threw back his head and laughed. "Feel sorry for you, Roz? A woman like you would never warrant feeling sorry for."

"A woman like me?"

His eyes traveled down the length of her. "You've never been a little flower that wilted under stressful conditions."

Rozlyn's mouth twisted to a wry smile. "I never had the opportunity to be a flower."

Jack eyed her thoughtfully. "Would you have liked that? To be a flower?"

She moved closer and leaned against the tailgate of the truck. "Not necessarily a flower," she answered. "But after Mother and Daddy died I didn't have much of a chance to be feminine. It's impossible to do ranch work in dresses and heels." She looked out across the open range, unaware of the wistfulness on her face. "When all my friends were talking about their prom dresses, I was scraping cow manure off my boots."

Jack understood how hard that must have been on her. It might have been different if Axton had been younger and able to do some of the physical labor on the ranch. But at the time of the Campbells' deaths Axton had been seventy-six. At least living with his aunt and uncle had given Jack some sense of security. Rozlyn had been forced to take on the job of an adult long before it should have been asked of her.

Her wry smile said that all of those memories had been put in the past and forgotten. "I wouldn't have made a very good flower anyway. But I guess you know that better than anyone, Jack.''

Something about her young face, the courageous tilt to her chin made him want to reach out and draw her close to him. He wanted to tell her that she was a flower. She was like an Indian paintbrush. Bright, beautiful and tenacious until it was taken from its original home. Then it quickly withered and died.

''I know better than anyone that under those clothes is a hot-blooded woman.''

Her heart jerked. ''Yes, only you would know that,'' she said in a low voice, then swallowed and looked away. ''Jack, do you think that—we could quit arguing and be friends?''

''Friends?''

She looked back at him. ''What else could we be?''

What else? He wanted to be her husband again. When he'd decided that he didn't know. Maybe he'd never really stopped wanting to be her husband. He wasn't sure anymore.

''Is that what you want?''

She nodded, her throat thick. At least it would be better than flinging hateful accusations at each other, she thought.

As he let out a heavy breath, his eyes narrowed on her face. ''I'm not your friend, Roz. I'm your husband. Maybe it's time we both remembered that.''

Rozlyn was so shocked that for several seconds she couldn't say anything. Eventually she gave a short laugh of disbelief.

"Jack you—don't mean that!"

He lowered his foot from the bumper to the ground and straightened to his full height. "What makes you think I don't mean it?" he asked.

The seriousness in his voice made her take a look into his eyes. She wished desperately she could read behind them, to see what he was really feeling. But she knew the answer she wanted to know could only be found in his heart.

"Because—I know you, Jack. And, if anything, what—happened between us this morning in the bedroom proved it. You don't want me. Especially as your wife."

Jack reached out and traced his finger along her jawline. "Rozlyn, in spite of our troubles, we had a lot of good times together."

Rozlyn started to tremble. "Yes, we did. I don't deny that." She couldn't deny that while they'd been together Jack had filled her life with bright warmth, excitement and love. It was those times he'd been away that she'd hated.

"I'm wondering if we couldn't have that again."

"I don't know how, Jack. I don't think either of us has really changed enough to make it work."

His hand dropped from her face only to pick up the braid on her shoulder. Rozlyn felt frightened by this new Jack. A softer, gentler Jack would be extra hard to resist.

"I've changed, Rozlyn."

Rozlyn wasn't sure she wanted to hear any more, but she had a feeling he would tell her anyway.

"You still look like the Jack I knew. You still talk like him. And you still behave like him."

He grinned at her, a lopsided grin that creased his left cheek with a deep dimple. "But I don't feel the same."

Rozlyn's heart jerked into rapid motion. A part of her wanted to ask him to explain; the other part was afraid to hear it.

Confusion, even wariness passed across her face and Jack knew he'd stunned her. Hell, as far as that went, he'd stunned himself.

"When I left here, Roz, I thought rodeoing would be enough. I thought my life would be full with my career. It isn't."

Rozlyn's eyes grew wide. "You love what you do!"

"Yes, I do," he conceded.

"You won't quit. You haven't quit. Have you?"

His gaze didn't waver from hers. "I'd like to ride until I'm thirty-five. If I'm lucky, I've got four or five years left of good riding."

Her heart plummeted, although she didn't know why. She should know better than anyone that Jack would never give up rodeoing until age forced him to. "I see," she said in a strained voice.

Quickly she turned and moved away from him. "I have soup and sandwiches waiting for lunch. I'd better get back and see that Axton eats."

"Rozlyn! I'm trying to talk to you."

She looked over her shoulder, then shrugged. "There's nothing to talk about. You plan to stay on with your career. You're not serious about being my husband."

Jack took one long stride and gripped her by the arm. "It *is* possible to do both. A lot of men do. But then I'm forgetting they have loving, supportive wives," he added bitterly.

Rozlyn jerked her arm from his grasp and stalked angrily back to the house. She wasn't going to let him use her again. He only wanted to be a husband when the urge hit him. That wasn't good enough for her.

"What's the matter with you, Sis?" Axton asked as Rozlyn banged through the back door of the kitchen.

She pulled out a chair at the dining table and slumped into it. "Pa, I don't know how much longer I can take having Jack around here!"

The old man shook his head. "I'll never figure you out, child. When Jack left the ranch, you wanted him back home. Now that he's finally come back, you want him to leave."

She dropped her face into her hands. "He hurts me, Pa. He hurts me inside and out," she said, her voice trembling.

The next moment she felt her grandfather's hand on her shoulder. The comforting gesture brought a sting of tears to her eyes. "Just what do you want from Jack, honey?"

Sniffing, she lifted her head. "I—used to want him

to—'' She shook her head, then started again. ''I wanted him to be here with me, to love me, to have children with me. Is that so much for a woman to ask for?''

''Jack's not like most men, Rozlyn. But you knew that when you married him.''

She nodded glumly. It was true she'd known he wasn't a conventional family man when she'd married him. But she'd thought all that would change once they were actually married. She'd hoped his love for her would be so strong he wouldn't be able to leave her for long days running. It hadn't turned out that way. And now he was expecting her to relive those days of feeling lonely and abandoned.

''He's not going to give up rodeoing, Pa.''

''You didn't really expect him to, did you?''

She shook her head, then looked up at her grandfather. ''Now he says he wants to be my husband again.''

Axton cocked a white brow at her. ''Well, are you ready to be his wife?''

Was she? Hadn't a part of her always been his wife?

''Oh, Pa, if—if I thought for a minute that he might still love me—I—'' She couldn't go on. It was both pointless and painful.

''What makes you think he doesn't?''

She stared at her grandfather. ''Well, it's pretty obvious, isn't it?''

Frowning, Axton shook his head. ''I guess you'd

see things differently if he'd said he wouldn't get on another bull.''

Her eyes widened as she weighed his suggestion. ''Of course I would. It would prove he was committed to me.''

Axton rubbed his chin thoughtfully. ''Well, Sis, if that's the case, and you think that Jack has to prove his love, how are you gonna prove yours?''

Rozlyn's back was suddenly ramrod straight. ''What?''

''You heard me. How are you gonna prove to Jack that you care about him?''

''I don't have to prove myself to him! If I ever told him I loved him, it would be because it was the truth.''

He clicked his tongue at her. ''Then why can't you take Jack's words at face value? Why does he have to give up something to prove his love to you?''

Rozlyn's mouth opened to speak, but suddenly nothing would come out. Jack had accused her of the same thing. Was she really looking at things from just her side of it? If she turned things around, how would she have felt if Jack had asked her to give up the ranch completely for him? But he hadn't, she thought dismally. She'd been the one doing all the demanding.

''I guess you were going to tell me that what's good for the goose isn't necessarily good for the gander,'' Axton drawled.

''Pa—the man doesn't want the Broken Spur to be his home.''

Axton reached out and patted his granddaughter's

cheek. "Honey, one of these days you're gonna see that home doesn't necessarily mean a house or the land it sits on. It means being with the one you love."

The back door opened and Jack stepped into the kitchen. He took one look at Rozlyn's guilty expression and said, "If you were talking about me, you don't have to quit just because I can hear it."

Axton looked at his granddaughter. "We were just talking about a goose and a gander. Rozlyn's not sure she wants a pair for the ranch yet."

Right now she wasn't sure about anything, Rozlyn thought dismally. "I'll think it over, Pa," she assured him, then got to her feet to put lunch on the table.

Chapter Seven

After lunch, Rozlyn steeled herself to go back to the barn with Jack. There were cattle to be fed, horses to be cared for. She had to put aside her troubling thoughts and focus on the work ahead of them.

Jack said little while they loaded the pickup with hay and feed. Rozlyn supposed he was still angry with her, but that was nothing new, she thought sadly.

"It's getting cloudy again," she remarked as she looked out the windshield. "I wonder if we'll have more rain."

Jack slowed the truck as he maneuvered it around a boggy spot in the dirt road. "I hope not, or it's going to be heck getting out here to feed," he said.

Rozlyn drummed her fingers against the seat. "Jack, I—" She broke off as she turned to look at him. "I want to thank you."

Jack's brows shot upward at the unexpected words. "Thank me?"

His disbelief had the corners of her mouth curving upward. "Yes, I do say thank you when I feel it's warranted. So I'm saying thank you to you."

"For what?"

"For helping me. I realize you didn't have to come back to the Broken Spur. It—it's been awful since Michael left," she confessed. "I was working so hard I could hardly hold my head up over the supper table. Your being here has taken a great burden off my shoulders."

"Thank you."

She dropped her gaze. "I know sometimes I seem ungrateful—but I do appreciate your help."

"Think nothing of it. I'd do it for any of my friends."

Rozlyn supposed she deserved his ire. However, his words still had the power to hurt her. "Well, as I said before, thank you."

Jack's frustration left him as he glanced over at her figure huddled in the corner of the seat. She really was being sincere, and it reminded Jack that underneath all her stubbornness and bravado was a vulnerable woman. She'd lost and suffered and struggled a lot in her young life. So had Jack. It was one of the reasons they should be together, he decided, why they should put aside their bitterness and make a life together.

"I didn't mean that, Roz," he said quietly. "I wouldn't do this for just anybody." His admission took her by complete surprise. She glanced at him, wondering what he was really trying to say to her. Was he trying to tell her that he cared about her? Really cared?

The idea brought a lump of tears to Rozlyn's throat, forcing her to look away from him and swallow. "Well, I'm glad you're doing it for me."

Things were changing between them, she realized. She could feel it, but she didn't know what to do about it. She didn't even know if she *should* do anything about it.

Rozlyn's thoughts were suddenly interrupted as she spotted a bull just off to her right. The black animal was standing beside a cluster of mesquite, his hindquarters twisted at an odd angle.

"Jack! Stop a moment!"

He pressed on the brake and looked in the direction she was pointing.

"It's my bull. He's not with the herd, and look at the way he's standing."

"You're right. I think we'd better go have a look," he said.

Instead of trying to drive over the mushy ground, Jack parked the truck where it was and they walked the hundred or so yards over to the bull.

The animal was obviously in pain. As Jack and Rozlyn approached it, the only movement he made was to turn his head and warily eye the two of them.

"Oh, Jack! His leg is mangled," Rozlyn gasped.

Jack saw it at the same moment she spoke. There

were deep slashes in the flesh above and below the hock and a major amount of swelling up and down the whole leg.

"I wonder how he did this? Do you have another bull penned in this pasture?"

Rozlyn shook her head. "No. In fact, he's the only bull I have."

Jack drew as near to the bull as he could for a closer look at the wounds. "Well, then he must have gotten into barbed wire or a thicket of some kind."

"There are so many cuts," Rozlyn remarked with dismay.

"That's usually what happens if they do get caught in some way. The more they fight to get out, the more they cut themselves."

"He needs medical attention, don't you think?" The sight of the wounded animal saddened Rozlyn. Not only because he was an asset to the ranch, but also because he was a helpless animal in pain.

Jack nodded, then straightened up. "You might lose him if he doesn't get it. Come on, we'd better go back to the barn and get the stock trailer," he told her.

For the next hour they worked to get the bull loaded and back to the barn. Shortly afterward the local vet arrived to examine him.

He was an older man with the patience of a saint where animals were concerned, although he never minced words with the people who owned them.

"He's chopped that leg up pretty good, Rozlyn. I'll

have to keep him at the clinic for at least a couple of weeks.''

"Two weeks! Dr. Grady, that's a long time. Couldn't Jack and I take care of him here?''

The tall man shook his gray head. ''You want him to live, don't you?''

Of course she did, but having the bull stay at the clinic for two weeks would be very expensive. ''Yes, but is two weeks necessary?''

He took his hat off and scratched his head. ''Now, Rozlyn, you know I wouldn't tell you something like that if it wasn't necessary. I'm going to have to do quite a bit of sewing on him, and then he'll have to be injected with antibiotics daily. I want him in the cleanest environment I can keep him in, and that doesn't mean this barn.''

''Dr. Grady's right, Rozlyn,'' Jack spoke up. ''You don't want to chance him getting infection in his bloodstream.''

Rozlyn knew both men were right. The loss of the bull would be far more difficult to overcome than a vet bill. Without the bull, there would be no calf crop in the months ahead. And without the income of a calf crop, the ranch would surely go under.

''Yes, I understand,'' she told the doctor. ''We'll bring him right over to the clinic.''

That night after supper Jack found Rozlyn in the den going over a stack of bills. Axton had already gone to bed, and the only light in the room came from the flames in the fireplace and the small lamp on the desk where Rozlyn was working.

Leaning a hip against the desk, he looked down at her. "You didn't want to leave the bull at the clinic, did you?"

Rozlyn had been so involved in her figuring that she was unaware he'd even come into the room. She looked up at him with mild surprise. "I wished it hadn't been necessary, but it was, so I'll just deal with it as best I can."

"I'm glad to hear you're not going to let it worry you."

She put her pencil aside, then rubbed her eyes. "I've learned that worrying doesn't fix anything."

Jack's eyes traveled over her bent head, the tired movement of her fist against her eyes, then on to the glossy fall of her hair against her back. Without thinking, he moved behind her, then reached out and lifted her hair in his hands.

"You know," he spoke softly, "I remember when I used to brush your hair for you."

Rozlyn's lips curved into a wistful smile. "I can remember you saying it was as coarse as a horse's mane."

He gave a low chuckle. "Yes, but that's because a horse's mane is very pretty when it's cared for." He slid his fingers gently through the long strands. "And your hair is still just as beautiful as it always was."

To have him touch her, even in the simplest way, was both a pleasure and a pain to Rozlyn. So much of her wanted him to keep on touching her, but the other, cautious part of her was still afraid to chance her heart on him again.

"I've been thinking, Rozlyn."

Her whole body was taut, statuelike as she anticipated his next move. "Oh? What have you been thinking?"

"That the ranch needs another bull."

Surprised, Rozlyn twisted around in the chair in order to see his face. "You heard Dr. Grady, Jack. He said the bull would be able to go back into service probably within six weeks."

"Any other time that wouldn't make a difference. But if you want the majority of your cows to calve next spring you need a bull on them now. Not six weeks from now. Besides," he said, leaving her side to take a seat on the couch. "You need more than one bull on the Broken Spur."

Rozlyn left her place at the desk to join him on the couch. Jack watched her carefully wrap the folds of the robe over her bare thighs. He could have told her that hiding her legs did little to get the sight of them from his mind.

"Jack, a bull is a big investment. I can't do it right now."

"But I can," he said, crossing his boots out in front of him.

Rozlyn was momentarily speechless. "And why would you want to? Are you—"

"Trying to buy my way back into your life?" he

finished for her, a dry twist to his mouth. "Roz, we both know your affection couldn't be bought."

At least he realized that, Rozlyn thought with relief. "Then why?"

"This ranch is just as good an investment as anything else. If it makes you feel better you can promise me two or three calves out of next year's crop."

Her green eyes grew soft as they roamed his face. "I'm beginning to think you really care about this place."

He'd always told himself he didn't. After all, it had been one of the things that had torn them apart. But coming back and finding Rozlyn struggling to save it was making him view the place in an entirely different way.

"I don't want you to go through what my mother went through, Roz. I'd buy a dozen bulls to prevent that from happening."

Rozlyn didn't know what to say. She looked across the room to the rocker her grandfather always sat in. In a way it was a symbol of everything she'd worked for over the years. A home and family that would always be. "You've told me often that you wished your parents had never tried so hard to hold on to their ranch."

Sighing, Jack pushed his fingers through his hair and leaned his head against the back of the couch. "Well, maybe I was seeing that from a child's eyes. I was thirteen. But that wasn't old enough to understand everything about adult life. I could only see that the struggle to keep it tore my family apart. Now I'm wondering if my father didn't try hard enough.''

Maybe *he* hadn't tried hard enough with Rozlyn, Jack continued in his thoughts. His father had walked when things got rough. Jack had walked, too. At the time it had seemed the only thing to do.

Rozlyn dragged her eyes back to Jack. As she took in the desolate look on his face, she felt as if a hand were pressing relentlessly between her breasts. Jack talked about his father not trying hard enough. Did he think she hadn't tried hard enough to make their marriage work? At the time Rozlyn thought she had, but now she wondered if she'd been trying in the right way.

Something compelled her to reach over and cover his hand with hers. The unexpected action brought his eyes over to hers.

"If you want to buy a bull for the ranch, then I'll be grateful," she told him.

Jack's heart swelled with unexplained emotions. He'd always wanted to do things for Rozlyn that would make her happy. Yet in the past he'd never seemed to get anything right. The look in her eyes told him he'd gotten it right this time.

The next few days Jack spent what spare time he had, between feeding cattle and building fence, in trying to find a bull. Most of the local ranches didn't have any for sale. The few that did were not the right breed to work with Rozlyn's Angus cattle.

That night after supper Rozlyn went to the den to find her grandfather playing another game of solitaire and Jack back on the phone talking to yet another cattle buyer.

Rozlyn curled up on the end of the couch and pretended an interest in the TV. But in actuality her attention was on Jack. Since the day they'd found the injured bull an uneasy truce had existed between them. He hadn't touched her or tried to make love to her since the morning they'd argued in the bedroom. The fact should have relieved her, but it didn't. Her mind was consumed by him, and each time she looked at him, she was overcome with a hungry, empty ache inside of her.

After a few more minutes Jack hung up the phone and turned around to give them the news. "I've found a bull," he said with a wide smile.

"Well, it's about time," Axton pointed out. "It's a hell of a disgrace to the state of Texas when you have to hunt for days to find one bull!"

Rozlyn ignored her grandfather's remark and looked over at Jack. "Where is it?"

"Houston. I told the man we'd be down to buy him tomorrow."

"We? I'm not going to Houston."

His grin was devilish as though he were enjoying the moment. "You will if you want a bull. I only know how to ride one, not buy one."

It had been ages since Rozlyn had been any distance from the ranch. And as for going all the way to Houston with Jack, she didn't know what it would do to her. They'd be confined in the cab of his pickup for hours on end. She'd be crazy by the time they drove all the way to Houston.

Quickly she looked to her grandfather for a way out. "Pa, tell him I can't leave you."

Axton frowned at her. "Margaret will have her nose right over here the minute you leave. I guess that old woman can see to my needs."

"Someone has to be here to feed," she insisted.

"I'll hire someone for a couple of days. That won't be a problem," Jack told her.

Knowing it would seem childish to argue about it, Rozlyn held her hand up in a gesture of surrender. "Okay. You two have made your point. I guess I'm going to Houston."

Jack was surprised at how easily she gave in, and the fact that she had broadened the grin on his face.

"Then you'd better go pack," he told her. "We'll be leaving early in the morning."

When Jack said early, he meant long before daylight. It was still cold and dark when they left the ranch. Axton, who'd been up drinking his coffee and listening to the livestock report, waved them off with a gleam in his eye.

"You see that you get that bull back here safe and sound, son. I just heard cattle prices are higher than they've ever been," he told Jack before the two of them departed.

"I'll do that, Axton. And you won't need to worry about your granddaughter either. I won't let the big city swallow her up."

Axton cackled. "I'm not worried about Rozlyn. I expect the city would spit her back out if it got a taste of her."

"I don't know why I'm going to kiss you bye," Rozlyn told him as she smacked a kiss on his wrinkled cheek, "when you talk about me the way you do."

"'Cause you're a good girl, that's why," he said, fondly patting her arm.

Rozlyn was still remembering her grandfather's words long after they'd left the ranch and passed through Llano.

"Do you think Pa will be all right, Jack? I've never been away from him overnight since—well, long before you left the ranch."

Her words not only told Jack of how devoted she was to her grandfather. It also told him what little life she had for herself. Margaret had told him she rarely went anywhere other than to the feed or grocery store, or to church on Sunday. The birthday party the other night had been a big exception for Rozlyn.

Jack had always believed her lack of interest in outside life was because she was obsessed with the ranch. But now he wondered if he might have been wrong about that.

From the time Rozlyn had lost her parents at the age of sixteen, she'd been responsible for the care of her brother and her grandfather. It was something she hadn't necessarily asked for. But it had fallen onto her shoulders anyway. Then Jack had come along and expected her to put all that aside and go with him on the road. It had been asking too much of her, he supposed.

The realization hit him suddenly, causing his eyes to leave the road and turn to Rozlyn. The woman he'd married had always cared for others and never herself. And she didn't even know it.

The sun was high in the morning sky when they passed through Austin. Rozlyn looked out at the rolling hills dotted with scrubby cedar. "I'd almost forgotten how pretty the hill country is," she told Jack, her voice telling him how much she was enjoying the new scenery.

"I don't ever remember you saying you've been to Houston. Have you?"

She shook her head. "I never had any reason to go."

He didn't say anything to that and she looked over at him, her expression curious. "Why do you keep an apartment there?"

He shrugged. "I have to have some place to call my permanent residence. And since it's in Texas and located close to several PRCA rodeos, it's as good a place as any."

"But the city," she went on. "I can't imagine a cowboy like you living in the city."

He smiled at her. "Believe me, Roz. I don't live

there. It's just a stopping-off place to change my suitcase with a different set of clothes and to lick my
wounds if I have any. As for living, I do that on the
road.''

And he loved it, Rozlyn thought wearily.

''I'm fortunate in the fact that I have only myself
involved in the event I do,'' Jack went on. ''People in
the timed events like team roping and barrel racing
have to have some kind of acreage to keep their
horses, not to mention the work and expense it costs
them to haul animals cross-country.''

No, Jack thought, for the past two years he hadn't
had anything or anyone to worry about other than himself. But that was all changing. These past days he'd
spent on the Broken Spur had opened his eyes in ways
he hadn't expected, and he felt his life changing with
each new day. He knew now that he could never go
back to living as he had the past two years. What he
didn't know was how he was going to prove to Rozlyn
that their lives would be better if they'd put their marriage back together.

By midday they were traveling on I-10. At Colum-
bus Jack stopped for hamburgers. Although he didn't
hurry her, Rozlyn could feel his restlessness to be back
on the road, so she assured him she could finish her
milk shake in the truck.

''Are we behind schedule?'' she asked after he'd
merged back into the heavy interstate traffic.

''No. Not really. I told Mr. Donovan, the man

who'd be showing us the bulls, that it would be late afternoon before we arrived.''

''Oh. I got the feeling you were anxious to be back on the road.''

He looked at her with mild surprise, then a rueful smile spread across his face. ''I'm sorry, Rozlyn, I guess my old habits are showing through. I'm so used to pushing when I'm on the road, I guess I forgot we're not on a timetable.''

Frowning, she asked, ''Do you really have to push that hard?''

He nodded. ''Sometimes I have to travel hundreds of miles to make a rodeo one day and be at another the next. It may take eight, ten, or twelve hours of solid driving to get there in time to perform.''

Rozlyn was suddenly too ashamed to look at him. She was his wife. She should have known these things about his career. Rodeoing had always been a part of Jack's life. To think that before today, she'd never shown enough interest in his work to talk with him about it made her realize how narrow-minded she'd been in the past.

''I can't imagine traveling that far. It must be exhausting,'' she told him.

His smile was wry. ''It is. But what happens when I get there makes up for it. Earning several thousand dollars for eight seconds of work is rather thrilling.''

''It's also very dangerous.''

He cast her a sidelong glance. ''Living is dangerous, Roz.'' In fact, Rozlyn had hurt him far more than any bull ever had. Knowing that made Jack wonder if he was crazy for ever thinking of trying to be her husband again.

It wasn't much later that Jack turned off the interstate and headed south. Rozlyn, who'd been studying the road signs, looked at him in puzzlement. "Isn't Houston straight ahead?"

He nodded. "Yes. But the ranch with the bulls is southwest of the city, not far from Rosenberg."

Her eyes widened with interest. "Rosenberg. That's where you grew up."

"Yes."

"Do you know if the ranch your parents owned is still there?"

His shrug was evasive. "Not really. I've never felt inclined to look."

"Why don't we look today?" she suggested.

His mouth was suddenly a grim line. "We don't have time for it."

Rozlyn said nothing. She merely continued to look at him. Jack made a sound of frustration. "Look, Roz, the house probably isn't even standing now. Besides, I don't want to see it."

"Why not? I'd like to see where you grew up."

He glanced at her just long enough for Rozlyn to see the tight grimace on his face. "Because it will make me remember things I don't want to remember."

"Have you ever thought that might be good for you?"

He kept his attention fixed on the road. "About as good as being bucked off on my head," he muttered.

Rozlyn said nothing more, deciding it would be best to let the subject drop. She knew Jack had suffered as a child. Maybe seeing the old homeplace would be, for him, like revisiting an old grave.

She tried not to think of Jack as a vulnerable little boy feeling rejected and unloved. The image was too painful. Instead she focused on the land they were now passing through.

It was far different from the area round Llano. The trees, including an abundance of pecan, were far from scrubby. They towered into the sky and spread their limbs in wide splendor. Grass grew thick and green here, even though the last signs of winter could still be seen up in Llano. The ground, she noticed was mostly flat, but every now and then the highway curved as it passed over a little creek or rise. It was a lush, rich land. But it did not pull at her heart the way the starkness of West Texas did. But then, West Texas was her home and that, she supposed, was where the difference lay.

They'd been traveling for at least a half hour when Jack pulled the pickup to one side of the highway and killed the motor.

Rozlyn looked curiously around her. To Jack's left was a short driveway leading up to a simple wood-framed house. Other than that there was nothing around.

"I wonder where he keeps the bulls? I don't see any barns," Rozlyn remarked.

"This isn't the Donovan place. This was my home."

Surprise parted her mouth, but Jack didn't see her reaction. He was staring at the house.

Rozlyn scooted over in the seat closer to Jack so that she could have a better view from his window.

He turned to discover her chin nearly resting on his shoulder. For a long moment they looked into each other's eyes, both of them weighing and wondering. Jack's eyes were shadowed with the past. Rozlyn's, on the other hand, were filled with compassion.

"I didn't think you wanted to see it," she said softly.

"Neither did I until a few moments ago."

"And now?"

He turned his gaze back to the house. "It's almost like it was back then. Except it wasn't painted brown at that time. It was white. And Mama always kept red cannas growing by the porch."

There was a wistfulness to his voice that she'd never heard before. It tugged at her heart.

"Where did you run the cattle?"

"The land goes from that fence on the left, then back for three hundred acres. Behind that knoll the house sits on is where the barns and corrals were."

"I see," she said as her imagination placed a young Jack playing in the yard. "What about that big pecan tree in the yard. Was that there?"

A faint smile touched his lips. "Yes, although it wasn't nearly that big. I had to sit in a corner for two hours once because I broke off one of its limbs. That tree was Mama's pride. She used to talk about all the pies and candies she'd make when it started bearing pecans. I guess she never dreamed she wouldn't be there to pick them."

He turned back to Rozlyn. Something in his eyes compelled her to lift her hand and trace a gentle path down the side of his cheek.

"Sometimes things happen we simply can't control."

"Yeah. I know," he said, his voice little more than a whisper.

Rozlyn remained quiet as he took one last look at the house, then started the truck and drove away.

"I'm glad you showed me your old home," Rozlyn said after they'd traveled a few minutes.

"Well, at least I know it's still there. That it hasn't burned, or been torn down."

She studied his face, wondering what he was thinking. No doubt that his life would have been very different if his family had held together.

"I'm sure you had many good times there. You should remember those. Not the bad ones."

He looked over at her, and this time he smiled. Rozlyn was relieved to see it, and it dawned on her how much she wanted Jack to be happy. Did that mean she still loved him? God help her if it did.

"You're right, Roz. I did have many good times

there. I had a friend named Jim who lived about a half mile down the road from our ranch. We'd sneak off to the back pasture and ride the steers. When we knew Dad wouldn't catch us, that is," he added.

Rozlyn laughed. "Is that how you learned to ride?"

"Maybe it was," he said, laughing along with her. "Maybe a champion was made back there."

Chapter Eight

Rozlyn had a difficult time choosing the bull she wanted to take back to the Broken Spur. Since Jack had told her not to let money sway her decision, she eventually picked the one she believed had the best physical appearance and would remain healthy enough to service a large herd of cows. Once that was finished, Jack wrote Mr. Donovan a check and assured him they would be back in the morning to get the bull.

Darkness was falling over the city of Houston as the two of them entered the outskirts. The first thing that struck Rozlyn was the endless lanes of traffic. It was nothing like San Antonio, which she'd visited on rare occasions.

"I hope we don't have too much farther to go," she told Jack as he maneuvered the truck in and out of the heavy traffic.

Jack could see she was gripping the edge of the seat until her knuckles showed white.

"It's not very far now. Just relax. I'm used to driving in this."

Rozlyn forced herself to lean back against the seat. Her palms were sweaty and she wiped them down the thighs of her jeans as she looked over at Jack. "I guess I'm pretty much of a country bumpkin. You've probably been to big cities all over the United States."

"Quite a few."

"Everything is moving so fast. Pa would never believe this."

Jack laughed at the idea of Axton touring Houston. "I doubt Axton moved any quicker at the age of twenty-five than he does now."

A few minutes later Jack pulled into an underground parking lot. From there they rode an elevator up to his apartment, which was in a high-rise building.

Rozlyn's first impression of Jack's place was how impersonal the small unit of rooms felt. It was clean and modern and decorated in light tans and rusts, but it was lacking the warmth of day-to-day living.

"Have you thought about what you'd like for dinner?" Jack asked as he pulled off his hat and placed it on the bar that separated the living room from the kitchen.

Rozlyn placed her suitcase at the end of the couch, then turned to look at him. "Dinner? Oh, Jack, I'm so exhausted. Do we have to go back out right now?"

He wasn't surprised that she was tired. They'd had a long day, and she wasn't used to traveling.

"No. In fact, we don't have to go out at all, if you don't want to. I could have something brought up, like pizza."

She gave him a wide, grateful smile. "Pizza would be wonderful. I never get to eat it."

"If you're sure you wouldn't rather go out to a nice restaurant and have a big steak."

Shaking her head, she practically fell onto one end of the couch. "I raise my own beef, Jack. Believe me, pizza will be a big treat."

While he went to the phone to place the order, Rozlyn tugged her boots off, then leaned her head back and closed her eyes.

She must have dozed, because the next thing Rozlyn knew Jack was touching her shoulder and telling her the pizza had arrived.

Slowly she managed to rouse up to an upright position. "Gosh, did I fall asleep?"

"I think I could have set off a firecracker in here and you wouldn't have known it," he said teasingly, then motioned his head toward the bar. "Come on, I've fixed us a couple of sodas and the pizza's getting cold."

After a quick trip to the bathroom, Rozlyn joined him at the small bar. The aroma of the cheese and spicy meat made her mouth water as she took a seat on one of the tall stools.

"Mmm. Now this is easy cooking," she said pleasurably, after swallowing a small bite.

"I'm a very good cook. Even Axton says so," Jack said, grinning at her.

She took another bite. Beneath the veil of her lashes, she allowed her eyes to travel down the long length of him. He was wearing a black cotton shirt with his ever-present blue jeans. The dark color made his blond hair and gray eyes stand out in contrast.

Throughout the day it had been a struggle to keep her mind off Jack. But at least while they'd been traveling she'd had the varied landscapes and passing traffic to divert her attention. Here in this small, quiet apartment she could feel his presence reaching out to her. Need for him twisted inside her, and she wondered if this is what it felt like to be an alcoholic, desperate for a drink but knowing the end results would be disastrous.

"I'm so excited about the bull, Jack. He's a beautiful animal, don't you think?" She spoke to quell her struggling thoughts.

The sparkle in her eyes brought a smile to Jack's face. "Yes, I think you made a good choice."

She reached for her soda. "I think I'll give him a splendid name like Theodore, or Alexander."

"Why don't you just name him Bull Number Two? Since you already have one bull."

She made a face at him. "That would be demeaning, both to him and to my other bull. He already has the name of General."

"Oh, I didn't know that," he said.

"Have you ever ridden a General or a Theodore?" she asked.

He laughed. "No. The ones I ride are usually something like a Texas Tornado, Sweet Face, Raging Rambo. You know. Names with real personality."

Rozlyn was suddenly laughing so hard she nearly lost her breath. It was the first time since he'd returned to the Broken Spur that she'd laughed that freely, and it made Jack happy just to look at her.

The pizza was so rich Rozlyn could only manage two pieces. Jack continued to eat while Rozlyn finished the last of her soda.

"Jack, you're going to have to take several calves to pay for Theodore. I really wish we could have found a cheaper bull," she told him.

He shook his head. "I'm not worried about what I paid for him, so you shouldn't be either."

He stood up and began gathering the leftovers of their meal. Rozlyn helped with what little there was to do, then walked restlessly around the small living room.

By now it was very dark. Rozlyn parted the drapes and stared out at the city lights. They seemed to go on forever, like stars scattered over the ground. It was a beautiful sight, but one that made her feel very alienated. This was Jack's world. Not hers.

She heard his movements behind her and turned to see him sitting on the edge of the couch, tugging off his boots. The sight brought intimate images to her mind. Hot, sweet images that had her stuffing her hands down into her jeans pockets and swallowing at the tightness in her throat.

From the moment this trip had begun Rozlyn wouldn't let herself think about staying in Jack's apartment, about being entirely alone with him. But now she *was* alone with him, and the whole idea had her nerves drawn as taut as a bowstring. What would she do if he tried to make love to her? God help her, what would she do if he didn't?

"I—if there's something you need to do while you're here, or someone you need to see, I wouldn't mind staying here by myself," she said, trying to sound as casual as possible.

Jack's gaze followed her slim body as she moved restlessly around the room. "I have no reason to go out. Why? Are you trying to get rid of me?"

A few days ago Rozlyn would have been quick to anger at his question. Now she could only manage to give him a nervous smile. "No. Of course not. I just thought—you might have things you'd rather be doing."

Jack watched her through narrowed eyes and wondered if she was thinking the same thing he was thinking. That they were completely alone, with the long night ahead of them. "I think you're the one who'd rather be doing something else."

Realizing she was pacing, Rozlyn crossed over to the couch and took a seat at the opposite end from him. "I don't know what to do with myself when I'm away from the ranch,'' she admitted. Neither did she know what to do with herself when everything inside of her wanted to go to his side, to touch him as her lover and her husband.

''Well, there's plenty to do in a city of this size. There's the opera and the ballet, but it might be too late to get tickets tonight.''

Rozlyn knew he was teasing and she tried to laugh, but the sound came out more like a choked groan. ''Boy, wouldn't I look great at the opera in my boots and jeans?''

Jack's gray eyes were suddenly dark and serious. ''You look pretty good to me.''

The husky sound of his voice had her eyes going to his face. What she saw there caused her heart to pound heavily. The look in his eyes said he still found her beautiful, that he still wanted her. It was a look that both thrilled and frightened her.

Her eyes dropped away from his, and she clenched her hands tightly together in her lap. She was afraid if she didn't, she might reach for him and never let go.

''Jack, coming here to the city with you has shown me a lot of things.''

''What kind of things?'' he asked quietly.

''Oh, like how unsophisticated and coarse I am. How one-sided my life really is.''

Suddenly, he was beside her, prying her hands apart and holding each one in his own. ''Rozlyn, you could never be coarse,'' he said, his voice softly scolding.

She lifted her eyes to his. "I could never be polished. All I know about life is working cattle and horses. I—"

"You what?" he prompted when she failed to go on.

"I—don't really know why you ever married me."

His hands tightened on hers. "Roz! Are you crazy? I married you because I wanted you to be my wife."

"But I don't know why. I was just a little country girl who thought she knew all about life."

His lips twisted into a wry grin. "And what was I? A promising young lawyer? Or doctor?"

"Humph. I imagine you've made twice as much money riding bulls than a doctor or lawyer probably would have in their first years."

"Well, you didn't know that I'd be making that kind of money when you married me," he pointed out. "I was just someone who'd grown up without a family and you were someone who'd grown up trying to take care of one. Those were our only faults, Roz."

He released one of her hands, then reached up to push back the curtain of chestnut hair hiding her face. "And I think those are the only faults we have now."

She looked at him, her eyes searching his as she tried to understand what he was telling her. "Jack, we—"

He gently touched his fingers to her lips to stop her protest. "We made a mess of things, Roz. But we can change that. We can make it right. Starting now."

As his face grew nearer to hers, Rozlyn's green eyes

clouded with doubt. "How can we make it right, Jack, when—when—"

She didn't finish. She couldn't finish because his mouth closed over hers, blocking out anything else she had to say.

Until that moment Rozlyn hadn't realized how hungry she was for him. The taste of his lips, the touch of his fingers on her face stunned her with need.

Jack speared his fingers into her hair and pressed them against her scalp. His mouth feasted hungrily at hers. He heard her moan low in her throat, then felt her clutch at his shoulders. When her mouth parted wider, he thrust his tongue past her teeth and into the warmth beyond.

The intimate invasion sent heat coursing through Rozlyn's veins, making the blood pound in her ears until there was no sight, no sound, just the wild, delicious feel of him.

Needing more than just her kiss, Jack pressed her backward until both of them were sprawled at an angle on the cushions of the couch. He fumbled with the buttons on her blouse, while all the while his lips scattered kisses across her face. Rozlyn moved her hands restlessly against his back, then up to his collar where she pushed them into his short hair.

With the buttons of her blouse finally free, Jack pushed the two pieces of fabric aside and discovered her breast encased in white lace. Dipping his head, he covered the tip of one with his mouth.

Beneath the thin fabric, Rozlyn could feel his hot

tongue against her nipple, the pressure of his teeth as they sank into her breast. An aching need began deep inside her, then spiraled like a hot coil throughout her body. It left her mindless and greedy for the pleasure she knew he could give her.

Jack could feel her restless movement beneath him and knew she was asking for everything he needed to give her. Lifting his head from her breast, he pressed a quick kiss against her swollen lips.

"Not here," he said huskily, then stood and reached for her.

"Jack, no—" Sanity was trying to rear its head. "We can't—"

Before she could say more, Jack lifted her up in his arms and carried her out of the room. Rozlyn was unable to do anything but shut her eyes and lock her arms around his neck.

In the bedroom he placed her across the middle of the bed, then lowered himself over her, propping most of his weight away from her on one knee. "Let me undress you, honey," he whispered. "It's been so long."

Desire and a fatalistic acceptance of what was about to happen sent tremors throughout her body. To allow Jack to make love to her would mean giving her heart to him again. She didn't know if she was ready to take that kind of chance.

Her hands were shaking as they caught at his fingers, which were already easing down the zipper on her jeans.

A faint light from the living room slanted across the bed, illuminating the pale oval of Rozlyn's face. Jack could see the hesitancy in her eyes, yet he could also see passion clouding their green depths.

"What is it, my darling?" he asked, pressing warm kisses near her ear and along the tender column of her throat.

"I—I'm not protected," she finally managed to say, though it was impossible to explain that it was her heart she was really worried about.

He lifted his head and looked down at her lovely face. And suddenly he knew without doubt that his heart belonged to her. It had probably always belonged to her, he'd just refused to face up to the truth of it.

"It doesn't matter," he told her. "If our making love produces a child, it would be a precious gift."

Did he really think so? She wanted so badly to believe him. "Jack, are you sure?"

"Oh Rozlyn," he groaned, reaching up to frame her face. "Of course I'm sure. We need each other. Like this. Forever."

Forever. Did Jack realize what forever meant to her? "Jack—" she began in a fevered voice, only to have his mouth silence the rest of her sentence.

"I don't ever want us to be apart again, Rozlyn. Kiss me. Touch me. Show me that you want the same thing."

His mouth returned to hers. This time his kiss was hot and plundering. Rozlyn was breathless when he pulled away to shrug out of his shirt. When he had tossed it to one side, she reached greedily for him. She slid her hands up his rib cage, then across his hair-roughened chest.

While her hands continued their explorations, Jack slowly and methodically removed her clothing. When the last piece was tossed aside, he stood back to view his handiwork. Rozlyn felt her whole body blush under his scrutiny.

"Why are you looking at me like that?" she whispered.

"Because you are the most beautiful thing I've seen in a long, long time," he said, his eyes adoring her luscious body.

Quickly he removed his jeans, then joined her on the bed, drawing her body against his hard length. Rozlyn could no longer hang on to the doubts that had held her apart from him. She couldn't think of doubts and fears when his hands were touching her with sweetness and fire, filling her mind with nothing but pleasure.

This man was her husband, and no matter how hard she tried to forget him and push him out of her heart, she could no longer deny that she wanted him back in her arms, back in her life.

And when his mouth claimed hers once again, she tried to tell him with her kiss exactly how much she'd missed him and how much she still wanted him.

Rozlyn's eagerness drove Jack's already taut body nearly to the breaking point. His hands slid over her creamy breast, then down to her bottom where he tugged her hips closer, fitting her against his blatant arousal.

The intimate proof of his desire made the hot ache in Rozlyn too much to bear. Pushing his shoulders against the mattress, she straddled him, her long hair brushing his chest as she bent her head to kiss him.

"Jack, you taste so good, feel so good," she whispered feverishly against his lips. "Is it that way for you?"

"Oh, Rozlyn, my darling," he murmured, his voice hoarse. "Let me show you. Come here and be my wife again."

His hands moved to her hips to guide her downward, then with one deep thrust he was inside her.

Rozlyn's head reeled with pure ecstasy as he filled her body and her heart. Jack, on the other hand, had lost all conscious thought but the hot, velvety warmth of Rozlyn's body surrounding him, loving him. Finally she was his once again.

Searing passion quickly enveloped them both, bringing their bodies together in a hard, fast frenzy that brought cries from Rozlyn's lips and sweet, urgent words of adoration from Jack.

Then suddenly everything tightened inside her, the room tilted crazily and her hands reached out to hold on. Jack found them with his, sliding his fingers in between hers, then locking them tightly together. Their ride to heaven was quick and soaring. The spiral back to earth came much more slowly.

When Rozlyn's awareness did finally return, she

discovered she was sprawled on top of Jack, her face pressed tightly against the side of his neck. Her breathing was still rapid and her fingers remained tightly clenched with Jack's.

Beneath her, Jack wasn't sure if he was still alive. His heart was thundering in his chest, his senses reeling with the aftermath of their lovemaking.

With a groan Rozlyn raised her head to look down at his face. "I should move," she said, her voice tender and husky.

Jack released her fingers in order to fold his arms around her waist. "I don't want you to move. Ever."

Smiling, she reached out to run her fingers through the hair tousled over his forehead. His arms tightened around her, and for long minutes neither of them spoke as they let their bodies recuperate. Rozlyn closed her eyes and rested her cheek against the gentle rise and fall of Jack's chest.

The sweet familiarity of lying in his arms was almost as overwhelming as making love to him. Rozlyn wondered how she'd ever existed these past two years without him.

She moved in his arms to press a kiss against his shoulder. Jack looked down at her. He splayed his fingers against her back, then slipped them slowly up. Her skin was creamy white and soft as silk.

"I think I must have died. Is this heaven?" he murmured.

Rozlyn sighed contentedly and nuzzled her cheek

next to his. "It's heaven to be with you like this, Jack," she said, knowing it was the utter truth.

Rozlyn was still asleep the next morning, when Jack stepped out of the shower. After knotting a towel at his lean waist, he walked quietly to the side of the bed and looked down at her sleeping figure.

She was lying on her stomach with one knee drawn out to the side, her hands resting on either side of her head. Her curly hair tumbled in wild disarray down her back and partially hid the soft pink flush on her cheek.

All sorts of emotions swelled in Jack's heart as he watched her sleep. She'd loved him so completely last night, giving herself to him as though she were certain of him and the way she felt about him. But now that morning had come, Jack wondered if she would still feel the same way. She hadn't spoken the word *love* to him, but then neither had he spoken it to her.

Rozlyn had told him that where love was concerned, actions spoke louder than words. And he was beginning to understand what she'd meant by that. His mother and father had often spoken the word *love,* but ultimately their actions hadn't backed it up. He supposed Rozlyn had felt the same way when he'd spoken the words *I love you* yet had not stayed around long enough to show her that love.

The ringing of the telephone interrupted his thoughts. With one last glance at Rozlyn, he turned to go answer it.

Rozlyn woke slowly. When she first opened her eyes, the strange room disoriented her, then the events of the previous night came rushing back to her. She and Jack had made love. Not once, but throughout most of the night.

The memory brought a warm flush to her cheeks as she pushed back the covers and swung her legs to the floor. At first glance she didn't see her clothes, so she reached for Jack's black shirt lying at the foot of the bed.

She found Jack in the kitchen, sitting at a small glass table with his back to her. On quiet tiptoes she came up behind him and slid her arms around his neck.

"Good morning," she purred in his ear.

He instinctively reached up to caress the arms she'd locked over his chest. "Good morning."

Smiling, she nuzzled her cheek against his. "Are you going to cook me a big breakfast?" she asked teasingly. "I'm starving."

"I don't have any groceries in the apartment," he said.

"Oh, well," she said cheerily, "you can take me to one of those places where they have a breakfast bar with everything on it. I'm going to be a pig this morning."

"That'll be fine," he said, his voice strangely vacant.

Rozlyn quickly straightened away from him. "Jack? Is something wrong?"

The timing of the telephone call he'd received couldn't have been more wrong, he thought. But there was nothing he could do about it now. "No. I was just thinking."

When he didn't elaborate, she walked around in front of him. The minute she looked at his face her heart went still. There was a look of pain on it that sent fear rushing through her. Was he already regretting last night? Was he trying to tell her that it had all been a mistake?

"Jack," she began softly, "are you—" Not knowing how to put it in words, she stopped and started again. "Have I upset you?"

His gray eyes grew soft and loving as he lifted his face to look at her. "Upset me? No, honey. Of course you haven't upset me."

Some of the pent-up breath rushed out of her and she smiled tentatively down at him. "Well, the way you looked a moment ago I—wasn't sure."

Wanting to reassure her, he reached out and hauled her onto his lap. "It's not you, Roz," he said gently as he searched his mind for the words to say to her.

Even though his arms were around her, she felt a chill of premonition. "Then what is it?"

Jack knew there was no way to soften it, so he jumped in feetfirst. "I had a phone call a few minutes ago. It was from one of my rodeo buddies."

He didn't need to say any more. Rozlyn knew exactly what was in his mind and what he was trying to tell her.

''He said he'd been calling the apartment for the past few days to see if I was going to California this week.''

''Oh, I see,'' she said dully. She knew she should get up and put some distance between them, but she couldn't find the strength to do it.

''It's a big rodeo,'' he went on, eager to explain and hoping she cared enough to listen. ''To place in it would get me off to a good start this year. Especially coupled with my win at Cheyenne.''

''I'm sure it would,'' she said quietly, while inside she was screaming with pain. It had only been a few hours ago that he'd made passionate love to her, that he'd told her he never wanted them to be apart again. Now he was already planning to leave. It told her exactly what she meant to him.

Her heart laden, she pushed out of his lap.

Jack watched her cross the room, her arms hugged tightly against her waist. His black shirt barely covered her thighs. The sight of their creamy softness filled his mind with last night and the incredible intimacy they'd shared. He didn't want to lose that. He didn't want to lose her. Didn't she realize that?

''Well, no doubt you told him you'd go,'' she said, her voice growing bitter. ''Now that you've gotten what you wanted from me you're ready to hit the road again.''

Stunned that she could say such a thing, Jack could only stare at her. ''Roz, that's the crudest thing I've ever heard you say.''

She swung back around to him, sending her long hair flying around her shoulders. "Is it? Well, maybe that's because the truth is sometimes crude."

Frustration propelled him from the chair and across the room to her side. "Honey, how could you think I could use you in that way?" he asked gently.

When she didn't answer, he reached out and took her by the shoulders. "Rozlyn, you knew I intended to go on riding. This shouldn't come as a surprise to you."

As their eyes met, her face came alive with anger. "You're right about that. It shouldn't be surprising. But for some idiotic reason I thought—" She'd thought perhaps that he really did love her. That this time things would be different. What a fool she'd been! "I thought you'd at least give me a few days before you—left again!"

Sighing heavily, he lifted his hand and smoothed it over her hair. He loved this woman so much, needed her so much. Would she never understand that? "Roz, this whole thing caught me off guard. I'd forgotten all about this particular rodeo. In fact, if Ron hadn't called in my entry for me, it would be impossible for me to go. That should tell you how much my mind has been on you."

"It was. Last night," she corrected. "Now it's moved on to more important matters."

Seeing he was getting nowhere, Jack threw up his hands. Hell, why would she even try to understand him, or his needs? he asked himself. She never had in the past.

"You haven't changed a bit, have you? I suppose you're going to hold sex like a weapon over me now," he said.

Tears welled in her eyes. "Oh, I see. Last night it was making love. Now it's back to being just sex." He couldn't have hurt her more if he'd slapped her.

"Rozlyn! That isn't what I meant and you know it!"

She couldn't bear to hear any more. Her heart was breaking to pieces. Brushing past him, she hurried out of the room. In the bedroom she quickly threw off his shirt and tugged on her jeans. Jack came in just as she was buttoning the waistband.

His eyes clashed with hers, then dropped to her bared breasts. The hungry look he raked over them burned her like a searing brand. Desperately she turned her back to him and reached for her blouse.

"Rozlyn, if last night meant anything to you—if I mean anything to you, we won't argue about this."

Her throat ached with tears, making it almost impossible for her to speak. Tilting her head back, she closed her eyes and tried to swallow down the pain. "No, I'm not going to argue with you, Jack. I'm just going to ask you to take me home," she said in an utterly defeated voice.

Deciding he would gain nothing by continuing to argue with her, Jack said, "We have to go by and pick up the bull."

Still unable to face him, Rozlyn asked, "Are you sure you have time for that now?"

There was no anger or sarcasm in her question. Rather she sounded flat and hopeless, as if the life had drained out of her. Jack almost wished she'd turn and yell at him. Anything would be better than what he was hearing now.

"Yes. There's plenty of time." And maybe later, he thought, after she had time to cool off and think about it, they could talk more rationally.

"I'll go to the bank Monday and get a loan to repay you."

She was trying to put distance between them again. Jack knew he couldn't let that happen. Not now. Not after the closeness they'd shared last night. "I don't want—"

She whirled around to him, still clutching the blouse against her naked breasts. "I said I'm going to the bank. It's the only way I'd accept him now."

Jack's eyes turned to gray ice as Rozlyn brushed past him on her way to the door.

"Now if you'll excuse me," she said, "I'm going to take a shower."

In the bathroom, Rozlyn quickly turned on the shower full force, then sank onto the side of the tub and burst into sobs.

On the other side of the wall, Jack tore off the damp towel he was wearing and flung it to the floor. Damn it all, what was he going to do? Back down? Tell her he wouldn't go to California? Then what would happen the next time he wanted to go to a rodeo? They'd be going through this same scene all over again, he thought sickly. And he couldn't live like that.

The drive home was silent torture for Rozlyn. She feigned sleep most of the time, but behind her closed eyes she relived the moments they'd spent making love. She'd never felt happier in her life than she had last night. But obviously it hadn't meant that much to Jack. He could take her or leave her at any time. Anytime a good rodeo called, she thought miserably.

By the time they reached Austin, Jack could no longer stand the silence, or the idea that he was losing Rozlyn again. "Roz, what do you want? For me to give up my career?"

She'd been staring out the window, her dry eyes tired and aching from the tears she'd shed this morning and the tears that still begged to be released. At the sound of his voice, she blinked, then turned to look at him. "What?"

"I said, do you want me to give up my career?"

She studied his profile as he turned his face back to the traffic. Jack give up his career? The question was ridiculous. Jack was a bull rider; to try to take him away from it would be pointless. It was easy for her to see that now. If he did leave the sport, he'd be miserable and she certainly wouldn't come out the winner.

"I want you to be happy, Jack. And if rodeoing

makes you happy then I understand.'' But that didn't mean it made it any easier to bear, she thought sadly.

''What would make me happy, Roz, is for you to say you'll go with me to California.''

She stared at him, her expression incredulous. ''For me to go? Jack, do you hear yourself? I can't just take off—leave the ranch.''

''Somehow I knew you'd say that,'' he said, his voice heavy with sarcasm.

Stung by his attitude, she said, ''Unlike you, I have responsibilities that I can't just walk away from.''

''Oh, yeah, that's right. I'm like my father, aren't I? The irresponsible bastard who didn't love anybody but himself.''

''Jack,'' she began, only to stop as he turned an icy glare on her.

''I just wonder where I come in on your list of responsibilities?'' he asked cuttingly. ''Last? Or did I ever make the list?''

Rozlyn couldn't answer his questions, she was too angry, too hurt to speak another word. She was sick of hateful words, she was sick of deluding herself into thinking he might someday really love her. It was over this time, she thought dully. Really over.

Chapter Nine

Rozlyn went to bed early that night, so drained that she was certain she would fall asleep instantly. But it didn't work that way. She tossed and turned from one side to the other, then stared wide-eyed at the ceiling.

Jack would be leaving in the morning. He'd already packed his bags. She didn't know if she could bear seeing him go again. These past few days he'd been on the ranch had changed her life. It had shown her that she'd only been existing while he'd been out of her life. Was she to go back to merely existing again?

The question tormented her. Without even realizing it, she rolled onto her side to look at the door leading out to the hallway. Jack was only a few steps across from her room, and she couldn't help but think they should be sharing the same bed, making love to each other.

Should she go to him, tell him that she would leave the ranch and go with him tomorrow? Maybe her grandfather was right. Maybe home wasn't a house or a piece of land. Maybe it was rather a contentment of the heart.

But how could she be happy living on the road, hurrying from one city to the next? How could they raise a child in that kind of environment?

The questions were still haunting her when the ringing of the telephone pierced the quiet darkness.

Who would possibly be calling at this hour? she wondered. It had to be midnight, at least. Without wasting time fumbling around for her robe, Rozlyn ran in her nightgown to the kitchen to answer it.

As soon as she heard the strange voice on the other end, she felt a terrible sense of foreboding. "Yes, this is Mrs. Rozlyn Barnett," she confirmed in answer to the caller's question.

"Mrs. Barnett, this is Mary Ortez, head nurse at Mercy Hospital in Las Cruces, New Mexico. We had a young man brought in about twenty minutes ago. His identification lists you as his sister."

"Michael!" Rozlyn barely whispered his name.

"Yes, a Michael Campbell."

"What—what happened? What's wrong with him?"

"He has a head injury. My report says it was an accident at the rodeo involving a horse."

Fear shot through Rozlyn like a bolt of lightning, leaving her whole body quaking. "How—is he? Is the injury serious?'' she blurted as she tried to gather herself together.

''At this moment your brother is unconscious and unresponsive. However, his vital signs seem to have stabilized in the past few minutes.''

Rozlyn's throat was so tight she could barely speak. ''What does that mean?''

''It's hard to tell right now. The doctors have ordered a brain scan. That should tell them more about the extent of damage that's been done. Does Mr. Campbell have any relatives here in New Mexico?''

''No, I'm—I'm all the family he has.''

''So will you be the one to notify in case of any changes?''

''I—yes, but I'm coming there. It will take a few hours but—if Michael—I'll be there as soon as possible,'' she finished helplessly, then hung up the phone.

She ran down the hall and straight into Jack's room. Apparently he hadn't been asleep, either, because he spoke her name as soon as she started through the door.

''Rozlyn? What is it?'' he asked, raising up on one elbow.

Rozlyn rushed over to the side of the bed. ''Jack— oh God, Jack, Michael's been hurt! That was the hospital calling. He's—unconscious—it was a horse and—''

He bolted up in the bed, then tugged Rozlyn down

beside him. "Roz! Calm down and tell me slowly," he ordered. "Where is Michael?"

She drew in a ragged breath. "In—New Mexico. Las Cruces. A nurse called from the hospital." She stopped to gulp in another breath of air and realized her hands were shaking uncontrollably. "I told her I'd be there as soon as possible. I—I'd better go see if I can get Margaret on the phone. Someone will need to look out for Pa."

"You know I'm going with you," he said soberly.

Rozlyn was so close to breaking down, all she could manage to do was nod.

Jack couldn't bear seeing the horrible fear and anguish on her face. With a helpless groan he pulled her into his arms and crushed her tightly against him. "Don't worry, honey. We'll get there, and Michael will be fine."

Rozlyn could only cling to him and pray that he was right.

The drive to Las Cruces took them through the remainder of the night and well past lunch the next day. Midway through the trip, they stopped to call the hospital to find out if there'd been any changes in Michael's condition. The nurse Rozlyn talked to wasn't able to give her much information except that her brother was still unconscious.

Rozlyn was dazed with exhaustion by the time they reached the hospital, but fear for Michael kept her on her feet as they entered the medical building. They found her brother in the intensive care unit. Tubes and all sorts of monitors were hooked to him. Rozlyn had to fight back tears as she looked at him lying so pale and lifeless. Normally he was a bundle of energy, always finding something to laugh about. She couldn't imagine all that life suddenly ending.

As Jack stood beside Rozlyn, he was remembering the way Michael had looked down in San Antonio. He'd been so excited about riding broncs, so eager to rush out and prove himself as an athlete and a man. Jack had seen a bit of himself in Michael that night. Now he was seeing what it could have been like for him if he'd been the unlucky one. Jack's riding had caused him to lose Rozlyn. But in Michael's case it could be his life.

Rozlyn gently touched Michael's hand, his forehead and cheek, then looked back to Jack. "He—looks so awful," she said, her voice full of anguish.

Jack put his arm around her and led her out of the small cubicle. "Come on, honey. Let's see if we can find out more about his condition."

After talking to Michael's doctor, they knew little more than what they'd already been told. Head injuries were very unpredictable, the doctor told them. Once the swelling in the brain receded, Michael could be perfectly fine, or he could have permanent damage. It was too early for him to say.

The two of them spent the remainder of the day in the waiting area. During that time, several of Michael's rodeo friends came to check on him. They told

Rozlyn that Michael's horse had reared up and fallen sideways in the chute, somehow causing Michael's head to hit the iron fencing.

Rozlyn was glad to find out how the injury had happened, but the knowledge did nothing to take the fear and worry out of her heart. She'd already lost her marriage to the rodeo. She couldn't bear to think that her brother might never come back to her because of it.

By six o'clock there was no change in Michael's condition. Jack finally persuaded an exhausted Rozlyn that she should leave the hospital to eat and find a motel room.

"You're dead on your feet, Roz. You're not doing Michael any good by wearing yourself out," he told her as the two of them climbed into his truck.

"Yes, but he might wake up," she insisted, "and I wouldn't know or be there to see him."

"We'll call and leave a number with the hospital as soon as we find a room," he assured her.

They ate a quick meal at a fast-food place, then found a motel room as close to the hospital as possible. When they entered its small interior, Rozlyn's eyes went straight to the double bed. It would have made things simpler if there'd been two beds, but she wasn't going to make a fuss about it. She doubted Jack wanted any part of her. She knew if it wasn't for his love of Michael, he would have already been on his way to California by now.

After kicking off the pair of flats she'd worn, she

lay down on one side of the bed. Jack went straight to the phone and dialed the hospital. Once he'd hung it back on its hook, he took a seat at the foot of the bed and pulled off his hat.

"Sorry about the bed," he said stiffly. "It was all they had."

"There's no need to apologize." She knew he didn't want her that way, at least not since she'd refused to go with him to California.

His hat dangled from his hands as he rested his arms across his knees. "The hospital promised to call if there's a change in Michael. So why don't you get some sleep?" he suggested.

Rozlyn knew that Jack had to be exhausted. He'd driven over six hundred miles with only a few brief stops in between. And he'd done all of that without sleep. She was grateful to him, but she knew better than to read too much into the fact. He was here because of his concern for Michael, not because he loved her.

"You need to sleep yourself," she said.

He looked over his shoulder at her. "Yeah, I guess I do."

Rising to his feet, he walked over to the corner of the room and placed his hat on top of a portable television set. Rozlyn's eyes remained on him as he returned to the bed and began to tug off his boots. He was so strong and vibrant and alive. Yet one mistake in a bull ride could take all of that away. The thought was devastating to her.

"You know, Jack, it could be you lying up there in that hospital," she said as he stretched out on the vacant spot beside her.

"I know, Roz. It's something that I've always known." He settled his head on the pillow, then looked over at her. "But a person can't live his life dwelling on what might happen. Michael could have been just as easily hurt in a car accident," he reasoned.

Rozlyn sighed. Jack was right to a certain extent. Her parents' death was proof of that. "I know that, but—"

His eyes held hers. "But what?"

She'd been about to say that she didn't want to see anything like this happen to him. "You have to admit that what you do is extremely dangerous."

"You never seemed to worry about that part of it before," he said.

"Oh, I worried about it. I just never told you I did. I knew in the end my worrying wouldn't stop you from doing what you wanted to do anyway."

He remained silent as he thought about what she'd just said. Across from him, Rozlyn stared at the ceiling, thinking how quickly and dramatically things could change in a person's life. It seemed only a short while ago that she and Jack had been in Houston. They'd shared the same bed there, too, but in an entirely different way.

Instead of loving and comforting each other now, they were both lying stiffly away from each other. The inches separating their bodies might as well have been a mile.

"And what if that were me in that hospital bed now, Rozlyn?"

The question bewildered her. She turned to look at him as she tried to think of how she could possibly answer without exposing her heart. "Jack, please don't make me think of such things right now," she said wearily.

His gray eyes searched hers. He was fighting the urge to reach over and draw her to him. He needed to hold her close again, to feel her alive and warm in his arms. He needed to know that she loved him. That if his life were in danger she would care enough to come to his bedside.

"I just wanted to know—"

The ringing of the telephone halted his words. Rozlyn rushed to answer it.

"Is it Michael?" Jack asked the moment she hung it up.

Her face was suddenly wreathed in smiles. "He's regained consciousness and he's asking for us."

"Thank God," Jack said, quickly rising and grabbing his hat.

Back at the hospital they found Michael groggy but very happy to see them. He remembered the horse falling with him, but nothing afterward. Rozlyn was so relieved to see him moving his arms and legs and talking normally that she burst into a flood of tears.

"Well, gosh, Sis," Michael said, "I thought you'd be giving me a good yelling at."

"Your sister has been very worried about you," Jack told him.

"Shoot, I've had worse hangovers than this," Michael said with a weak grin for his sister.

She dabbed her eyes with a tissue then attempted to give him a scolding look. Yet it was impossible to do when she was so happy to see him awake and on the mend. "A hangover from what, buddy?"

Michael chuckled, then with a grimace rubbed the side of his head. "Ooh, I don't think I'd better laugh just yet."

"I don't think you'd better do anything but sleep right now," Jack told him, then turned to Rozlyn. "We'd better go and let him rest. The nurse said no more than ten minutes."

She nodded at Jack, then kissed her brother's cheek. "I hope this has taught you a lesson," she told him.

"Oh, it has," he admitted, his expression sheepish. "If I ever draw that horse Gray Witch again, I'm gonna run the other way."

Rozlyn shook her head in disbelief. She knew Michael was aware of how close he'd come to being killed, yet he still intended to go on rodeoing.

Jack patted his shoulder fondly. "You'll make it, boy. Someday you'll be telling your grandchildren how you rode in the National Finals at Las Vegas, Nevada."

A wide grin spread slowly across Michael's face.

"You don't know what it means to me to hear you say that, Jack. To know you still believe in me after this, makes me feel a whole lot better."

Jack gave Rozlyn a teasing glance. "Well, don't tell anybody, Michael, but your sister got bucked off the other day, too."

Michael looked totally shocked. "Did you, Rozlyn? I can't believe that!"

Rozlyn gave Jack a dry look. "I knew you'd have to tell somebody."

Michael laughed again before he happened to remember that it would make his headache even worse.

Rozlyn said defensively, "I was on Buster, and the weather was cold. It could have happened to anybody."

"I know one thing," Michael said on a long sigh. "It sure is good to see you two back together again. I knew you both still loved each other. Seeing you here together like this is almost worth getting hurt for. Maybe I'll be getting a niece or nephew soon."

There was such a look of happiness on Michael's face that Rozlyn couldn't bear to tell him the truth, at least not tonight. "You're getting tired," she said, "we'll come back to see you in the morning."

Both Rozlyn and Jack remained quiet on the way back to the motel room. All sorts of mixed emotions were running through Rozlyn as they drove the short distance. On one hand she was feeling utter elation that her brother was awake and seemingly had the use of all his faculties. On the other hand she knew Jack would be leaving soon. Now that Michael was improving there was no reason for him to stay. And the fact was breaking her heart.

"Well, it looks as if Michael will be good as ever in a few days," Jack said as they entered the small motel room.

Rozlyn sat down on the edge of the bed while Jack carefully locked the door behind him.

"Yes, thank God. I wonder how long they'll keep him in the hospital?"

Jack moved away from the door and came to stand in front of her. "That's hard to say. Depends on how well the doctors think he's doing. Probably not long."

Rozlyn bent her head back in order to see his face, and for the second time that night she felt tears burning her eyes. "Well, it doesn't really matter. You still have time to make it to California before the weekend."

His face grew strangely expressionless. "Is that what you want? For me to leave?"

Rozlyn felt as if someone had a hand on her heart, squeezing it tighter and tighter until she could no longer breathe. "Don't ask me that, Jack. It hardly makes any difference now."

Unable to face him, she rose to her feet and crossed to the other side of the bed. With her back to him, she said, "No matter what I said, it wouldn't make any difference. I know that you want to go, and I know now that it wouldn't be fair of me to ask you to stay."

Tears brimmed over the rim of her lashes and fell onto her cheeks. She didn't attempt to stop them. For years, she'd had to be tough and strong, even when she'd felt terribly frightened and alone. It didn't matter anymore if Jack believed she was a helpless woman who needed him. She *did* need him. She could no longer pretend otherwise.

Like lightning, Jack was around the bed and taking hold of both her shoulders. "Roz, did I hear you right?"

She focused her watery gaze on his face. "About what?"

"That it wouldn't be fair of you to ask me to stay. Did you really mean that?"

She gave a single nod of her head. "Yes, I did. I guess that's hard for you to believe, coming from me. But not until tonight when Michael talked about riding again, after coming so close to being killed, did I realize just how much he loved the sport, how much you really love it. I have no right to ask you to give it up. I shouldn't have ever asked it of you. But—"

"But what, Rozlyn?" he whispered urgently, his fingers tightening on her shoulders.

"But I loved you so much, Jack. I guess—I was greedy. I wanted all of you for myself. I couldn't see that I was driving you away with my possessiveness."

Jack shook his head ruefully. "It wasn't all your fault, Roz. It was mine, too. I should have realized what I was asking you to give up. The Broken Spur, Michael and Axton, they'd been your whole life up until we married. Maybe in a way I was greedy, too. I wanted you with me, not stuck on a ranch, struggling and worrying over it, like my mother did.''

He reached up to tenderly frame her face with his hands, and Rozlyn could not stop the hope that was suddenly burgeoning in her heart. ''Roz, if you're not asking me to give up rodeoing, what are you asking me? Tell me what you want, honey,'' he said softly.

She threw her arms around his neck and held on to him in a fierce grip. ''I want you to be my husband again, Jack. Now and forever.''

His eyes squeezed tightly shut, he bent his head and buried his face in the side of her neck. ''Oh, Rozlyn, I love you. I don't think I knew what love or a family really meant until I married you. And even then I didn't know what to do with either of them. Can you forgive me for these past years?''

''Oh, Jack,'' she said, her words muffled by his shirt. ''Can you forgive me?''

He pulled her head away from where it was buried in his shirt. ''All I need to know, Roz, is that you love me. Do you?'' he asked, his gray eyes searching hers.

''I kept telling myself I hated you, Jack. I truly believed that I never wanted to see you again. But then when I looked up and saw you that day in the barn, I knew I'd been lying to myself.'' Awed by the depth of her feelings, she lifted her hand and touched his face. ''I love you, Jack. Love you with everything inside of me.''

Wondrous joy lit his eyes and spread his mouth into

a wide, beautiful smile. "We've been crazy, Roz. But we're going to make up for it."

"I didn't think I'd ever be saying this, but I'm glad Michael left the ranch when he did. Otherwise he would've never run into you down in San Antonio."

Jack shook his head. "Even if I hadn't seen Michael, something would have eventually brought me back to you. I was so unhappy. It was crazy that I'd won the world championship and was still miserable. But I wouldn't let myself believe that it was because of you. Seeing Michael again was only an excuse to do what I should have done a long time ago. Come home to you."

Groaning, she pressed herself closer to his warmth, his love. "You're right, Jack. We've both been foolish. We've wasted precious time—"

She broke off abruptly as his fingers began working loose the buttons at her throat. "Jack? What are you doing?"

His grin was sly, the light in his eyes wicked. "Making up for lost time. Remember, Michael thinks he's going to get a niece or nephew soon. We don't want to disappoint him."

He pulled the sweater over her head, then lifted her back onto the bed.

"But Jack, what about California? The rodeo you didn't want to miss?" she asked as he joined her in the middle of the bed.

Planting a hand on either side of her head, he brought his face down to within inches of hers. "It only takes a matter of minutes to fly to California from here," he said, his expression serious. "I've already hired Connie's husband to take care of the cows. And Margaret is taking care of Axton. We can stay here with Michael two or three more days, and still make the rodeo this weekend. Will you go with me, Roz?"

A tender smile tugged at the corners of her mouth. "You know," she began softly, "Pa told me that home meant being with the one you love. I know what he was trying to tell me now."

Reaching up, she pulled his head down to close the fraction of distance between their lips. It was easier to let her kiss tell him that she'd go with him to the ends of the earth. Because he was her home. And she was home to stay.

Two months later Rozlyn and Jack were driving on Highway 71 back to the Broken Spur. They'd been to Montana this past week. Rozlyn had loved the mountains. Jack had loved the bull he'd drawn. It had been mean and wild and he'd ridden him like the true champion he was. And from the silly, teasing grins Jack kept giving her, Rozlyn suspected he was still on a high from the win.

"Are you ever going to come back to earth?" she teased.

He chuckled. "I'm happy to be going home. Aren't you?"

She smiled back at him, her lovely face telling him how much she loved and adored him. These past two

months they'd learned how to portion their time between the ranch and Jack's career. Rozlyn was dis-
covering that traveling with Jack was opening up a
new world for her and balancing her life in ways she'd
never known. "We had a good time in Montana. But
I can't wait to tell Pa all about it. And I'm dying to
get back on Buster. You know he's coming round a
lot better than I'd ever thought. Maybe I didn't make
a bad deal after all when I traded that old saddle for
him."

"Maybe you didn't," Jack said, a secretive little
smile playing on his lips.

Since the weather was warm now, Axton and Margaret were sitting under the shade tree when Rozlyn
and Jack pulled to a stop in front of the house. The
homecoming was noisy, as hugs and kisses were ex-
changed and bits of news recounted.

"Is that Michael's truck parked down by the barn?"
Rozlyn asked after things had quietened down somewhat.

"Sure is," Axton answered. "He drove in yesterday. I think he's down at the barn right now."

"I'll go get him," Jack said quickly.

Rozlyn, who was sitting on the grass at her grandfather's knee, started to rise and go with him, but Jack
motioned for her to keep her seat. "You stay here and
visit with your grandpa. I won't be long."

Once Jack was out of sight Rozlyn said, "Now, Pa,
while we were in Montana, Jack went to a lot of trou-

ble to buy you a pair of suspenders. So you better act like you like them.''

"Suspenders? Hellfire! I wanted a pair of gal-leg spurs!''

Margaret started to laugh. Rozlyn tried her best to scowl at him, even though she found it amusing that her grandfather wanted a pair of spurs fashioned in the shape of a woman's naked leg, complete with a garter on the thigh and a high-heeled boot on the foot.

"What would you do with a pair of spurs? You can't ride anymore.''

"A cowboy never gets too old to wear a pair of spurs. If nothin' else he likes to have them on his feet just to hear them jingle.''

Rozlyn reached up and squeezed his gnarled hand. "Next time, Pa, I'll make Jack find you a pair of gal-leg spurs. I promise.''

The old man grinned, then patted her head. Just as Rozlyn was about to rest her cheek against his knee, she heard voices coming from behind them. Swiveling her head around, she saw Michael and Jack walking through the yard gate. Behind them on a lead rope was a yearling colt. He was white with black spots splattered randomly over his shiny coat. He was the most beautiful animal she'd ever seen.

Rozlyn's mouth fell open as she continued to stare dumbfounded at the two men and the horse.

"Well, now, ain't this a surprise,'' Axton said gleefully. "I never seen that colt around here before.

Guess he must have wandered over here through a hole in the fence."

By now Rozlyn was on her feet, hurrying toward Jack and the colt. "Where did this—"

Her question stopped as Jack handed the lead rope over to her. "He's my gift to you, Roz. I couldn't get the people to sell Mighty Warrior back to me. So I figured the next best thing would be his brother."

Tears welled in her eyes as she looked from Jack to the colt, then back to Jack again.

"Well, Sis, don't you think you should at least thank Jack?" Michael prompted with a broad smile on his face.

Suddenly she was laughing and crying as she flung her arms around Jack's neck. "I love you, Jack. I love you."

And later, she thought as she pressed her cheek against his, she had a surprise of her own to give him. But the news that she was carrying his child could wait until tonight, when they were alone together. After all, there was plenty of time. Their life together was only beginning.

* * * * *

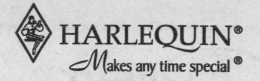

HARLEQUIN®
Makes any time special ®

HARLEQUIN®
AMERICAN *Romance*

Upbeat, All-American Romances

HARLEQUIN®
Duets™

Romantic Comedy

Historical, Romantic Adventure

HARLEQUIN®
INTRIGUE

Romantic Suspense

Harlequin Romance ®

Capturing the World You Dream Of

HARLEQUIN *Presents*~

Seduction and passion guaranteed

HARLEQUIN® *Super* ROMANCE®

Emotional, Exciting, Unexpected

HARLEQUIN®
Temptation.

Sassy, Sexy, Seductive!

Where love comes alive™

From first love to forever, these love stories are
for today's woman with traditional values.

A highly passionate, emotionally powerful
and always provocative read.

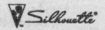

SPECIAL EDITION™

Emotional, compelling stories that capture the
intensity of living, loving and creating a family in
today's world.

INTIMATE MOMENTS™

A roller-coaster read that delivers romantic thrills
in a world of suspense, adventure and more.